The Exeter Blitz

The Exeter Blitz

DAVID REES

Hamish Hamilton
London

First published in Great Britain 1978
by Hamish Hamilton Children's Books Ltd
Garden House 57–59 Long Acre London WC2E 9JZ
Second impression January 1979
Third impression February 1980

ISBN 0 241 89759 9

Photoset, printed and bound
in Great Britain by
REDWOOD BURN LIMITED
Trowbridge & Esher

"We have chosen as targets the most beautiful places of England," said the German wireless announcer on the morning of May 4th, 1942. "Exeter is a jewel. We have destroyed it."

Exeter was not wholly a jewel. And the Germans did not wholly destroy it.

— from *Exeter Phoenix*, by Thomas Sharp.

For Lorna, Bob, Jon, Josie and Jenny
And with many thanks to Alan and Tom

Introduction

This story is not intended to be an exact reconstruction of the events in Exeter of the night of May 3rd–4th, 1942. The time of the raid, for instance, was about 1 a.m. on May 4th, not mid-evening of May 3rd; nor was there bombing on the previous night. The magnitude of the disaster, is, however, meant to be historically accurate.

In the first two and a half years of the war Exeter received little attention from the German Air Force. However, on March 28th, 1942, British aircraft destroyed the German port of Lubeck with incendiary bombs; there was very little purpose behind this raid other than testing a new method of aerial warfare, the fire-storm. Lubeck was of no strategic importance, but it was a place of great antiquity and beauty. Hitler, as an act of revenge, ordered that English cities of a similar nature should be bombed; Norwich, Canterbury, York, Bath and Exeter were the targets selected. These air-raids were nicknamed "Baedecker Raids", after the famous guide-book to places of architectural and historic significance.

Exeter experienced four "Baedecker" raids. The first three were on the nights of April 23rd, 24th and 25th. Eighty-one people were killed and one hundred and six seriously injured, but the damage to buildings was not extensive. The fourth and last occurred in the early hours of the morning of May 4th. For about an hour and a half German planes attacked, dropping large quantities of high explosives and over ten thousand oil and incendiary bombs, flying as low as five hundred feet to achieve accuracy. Their rear gunners relentlessly machine-gunned rescue workers, indeed anybody that could be seen. One hundred and sixty-one people were killed, and almost five hundred injured. The principal shopping areas of the city were left in ruins and most of the essential services, gas, water, electricity, sewerage, and the telephone system, put out of action. One thousand five hundred buildings were totally destroyed and nearly two thousand seven hundred severely damaged. The fire-storms that resulted were of an appalling intensity; the flames were visible thirty miles away, and they were almost uncontrollable, as fire-engines were unable to reach the scene owing to piles of blazing rubble blocking the streets. The public library burned so fiercely that it was still smouldering three weeks later.

The main architectural losses were the terraces of eighteenth century houses, Dix's Field, Bedford Circus, the upper part of Southernhay West. Bedford Circus was considered by many people to be the finest example in this country, outside Bath, of eighteenth century urban building. But the glory of Exeter is its cathedral, one of the great masterpieces of the European creative imagination. It is the only English cathedral to be built almost entirely in the Decorated style; it has the longest uninterrupted medieval vaulting in the world, and it is unique in that its towers were built on the transepts, rather than centrally, or at its west end. It survived with relatively little damage, though the city around it was flattened. Something of a mystery therefore remains concerning the air-raid of May 4th. The cathedral must have been (and still is) the most obvious target in Exeter from the air. Were the Germans just hopelessly inaccurate? Or were orders given that were disobeyed? Was it deliberately left more or less untouched? Why did the bombers not come back on another night, and finish their task? No-one has yet produced a wholly satisfactory answer to these questions.

The city returned to some semblance of normality with surprising speed. Within a week most essential services had been restored, and the majority of the homeless temporarily re-housed. Ways were driven through the rubble, and structures which were considered to be unsafe were pulled down. After the war the blitzed areas were rebuilt, but, though there is still much to see in Exeter that is both ancient and beautiful, what was lost in May 1942 was irreplaceable.

No resemblance, of course, is intended between people in the book, such as the Dean and the vergers, with their real-life counterparts in 1942.

The quotation from "Exeter Phoenix" by Thomas Sharp is reproduced by kind permission of the Architectural Press.

One

COLIN LOCKWOOD was bored and tired. There were three reasons for this, he told himself: it was an exceptionally warm afternoon; he had only had a few hours' sleep last night because of the air-raid; and Mr Kitchen, the history master, was being even duller and more aggravating than usual. Sixty or seventy people dead. No-one Colin or his family knew; most of the bombs had fallen on King Street, on Wonford and Pennsylvania, areas some distance away from where he lived. But the stories of what had happened had been filtering through all day. More than a hundred houses destroyed. An air-raid warden blown off his bike and thrown head-first into a sewage-pond, not a scratch on him; the only treatment he needed was a hot bath. A young mother, her arteries severed by flying glass. She had died before help could be fetched. A man blasted from his bed, hurled across the street, through a window, and into a room where a deaf old lady slept on, quite unaware of what was happening.

Why Exeter? There were no targets the Germans needed to destroy, no industry, no munitions factories, nothing. But it had a beautiful cathedral. That was the reason, people said.

He gazed out of the window. Lucky third-formers outside on the field, playing cricket! Pluck! The noise of ball on bat.

Pluck! A shout of excitement: someone had hit a six. If you hit a six that smashed the pavilion clock, the school presented you with the bat and ball to keep. No-one had ever smashed the pavilion clock, of course. And tomorrow, when he should be out on the field, when it was the turn of the fourth-formers, it would rain. He was sure it would rain. After all, it was only just May: afternoons like this were a surprise, a real bonus.

He rested his head on his arms, and looked at the new leaf-buds on the trees; when he half-shut his eyes they were like green dust in the slanting light, pale, as if they had not expected such sun, such heat. His sister Mary had a dress that colour. An expensive thing it was; it had taken most of her clothing coupons. He dozed right off.

He was woken by a sharp dig in the ribs. It was the boy who shared his desk, Terry Wootton. Colin disliked Wootton, who was an evacuee from London and who seemed to think, like all the evacuees from London, that he was in every way superior to the Exeter boys.

Colin sensed that something was wrong. The whole class was staring at him. There were a few grins of malice, particularly on the faces of the Cockneys.

"Go on! Answer!" Wootton hissed.

Mr Kitchen was leaning against the blackboard, idly throwing a piece of chalk in the air and catching it again. He looked distinctly unamused. Dangerous, in fact.

"Did you ask me a question, sir?" Colin ventured, timidly.

The class dissolved in laughter. "No, I did not," said Mr Kitchen, and added, sarcastically, "I hardly ever think it worthwhile asking a question of you, Lockwood, as I know perfectly well I shall never get an answer. At least, not a correct answer." The class guffawed obligingly. "As it so happens I was speaking to Wootton. I was merely wondering if he could explain why

2

you were fast asleep."

Colin glared at his neighbour, who was looking intently at his exercise book, a self-satisfied smile on his face. I'll wipe that smirk off your ugly mug, Colin thought; just wait till the bell goes!

"As you're wasting both my time and that of the whole class," Mr Kitchen went on, "I'll waste yours, Lockwood. You can write me a four-page essay entitled 'Why I am a fool'. No, boy! Not why *I* am a fool. I may well be one, but I'm not interested in your views on that. Why *you*" — and he jabbed his finger at Colin — "are a fool. And that's in addition to the homework I set just now. I suppose you were asleep then. Well, were you? Do you know what it is?"

"No, sir."

"So you'll just have to ask Wootton, won't you? Now, as I was saying before I was so rudely interrupted, in a city like Exeter there is history in every nook and cranny. Every stone has a tale to tell . . ."

Colin seethed with anger. Who did Kitchen think he was? So many members of staff had been called up in the last year or two that the school had gone to rack and ruin as a result. Aged buffoons, yanked out of their bath-chairs and wheeled in from their retirement bungalows in Sidmouth and Exmouth, attempted to go through the motions of teaching. The chemistry master, for instance, looked so old and wizened that rumour had it that he still believed in the phlogiston theory, had invented it maybe; but worst of the lot was Mr Kitchen: not only was he unbelievably old, but he had taught in London until he retired, donkeys' years ago, and so was always on the side of the evacuees. He was exceptionally good at revealing the dullness and thick wits of the Devon boys, and how the Londoners excelled them in intelligence and humour. He also had the weirdest ideas imaginable

3

about how to teach history. Instead of Acts of Parliament, dates of battles and reigns of kings and queens, he made his pupils study the old churches in the city, trace family trees and ask their grandmothers all sorts of idiotic questions about what they remembered of the Victorian Age. It wasn't history, to Colin's way of thinking, not real history like Fatso Gibbs had taught. No-one in the class would pass their exams at the end of the year. They would not have covered the syllabus.

There were supposed to be thirty-three boys in his class, but since the Londoners had arrived there were fifty-six altogether, most of them sharing two to a desk. There had been some tremendous fights, in the playground, in the classroom, on the way home, and the Cockneys had not always won, though their ways of fighting were underhand and vicious. He looked forward to putting Wootton in his place – he glanced at his watch – in exactly ten minutes' time. He wondered where Wootton was billeted. There were no evacuees with the Lockwood family; they had no room. Their house was small, old and inefficient, his father often said, adding, usually, that that was the penalty one had to pay for working for the cathedral. The Dean and chapter never had any money to spare on renovating church property. Dad was the cathedral's head verger, a job he loved, but it meant the Lockwoods had to put up with rising damp, floorboards riddled with woodworm, and a hot water system that almost blew up every time anyone ran a bath. Wootton probably lived somewhere with two toilets, one upstairs and one down, and a shower in the bathroom. He probably needed it. Half the Londoners had fleas and lice. Or so people said.

He suddenly remembered what the history homework was. That was a relief, not that he had intended to ask Wootton as old Kitchen had suggested. It must have been just before he

4

dropped off that the old fool had been burbling about it. And a more stupid impossible kind of homework would be hard to imagine. They had to produce by tomorrow — yes, tomorrow! — some relic or family heirloom, bring it to school and be prepared to talk about its age and significance. Significance be damned! There was nothing in the Lockwood household that was of any interest in that kind of way, nothing at all. Not even a photograph of Dad's grandparents, let alone the things old Kitchen was going on about, like samplers (whatever they were) or fire-irons or dairymaids' yokes. Dairymaids' yokes! He must think Exeter boys were all sons of cowhands, coming to school with straw in their hair and dung on their shirts. But, oh dear, *something* would have to be found. After today's little episode the old fossil would be certain to pounce on him.

The bell rang. Now for Wootton!

"Lockwood, just come here, will you?" What on earth did Kitchen want with him now? Wootton nonchalantly strolled out of the classroom, a delighted grin on his face, while Colin fumed, impotently. As soon as he was in the corridor Wootton would dash off at top speed and disappear, and there was nothing Colin could do about it. "I want to give you some paper for your essay," said Mr Kitchen, in tones that sounded genial, almost as if he was doing Colin a big favour, paper being in such limited supply what with the war and shortages and so on. "It's called foolscap. Not only very apt in the circumstances, you'll agree I'm sure, but it happens to be an extremely *large* kind of paper. None more so, in fact. Forty-six lines to a page." Colin gasped in dismay and Mr Kitchen smiled like a tiger.

It wasn't Colin's lucky day. Not only had Wootton vanished without trace, but everything at home seemed to conspire against him too. His younger sister June, with whom he normally got on quite well, who was in fact always ready to listen to his troubles with a sympathetic ear even though she was only ten, had brought her best friend, Pamela, home to tea. June and Pamela were an impossible combination for any male: separately they were quite ordinary, sensible people, more sensible really than most girls were, but together they turned into a pair of whispering, sniggering maniacs, bandying secrets back and forth, and if he was so foolish as to interrupt they would hoot and shriek with excited laughter, remembering some private joke about the clumsiness or the stupidity of boys and Colin in particular.

His mother, noticing his scowls, and fearing that Pamela and June would goad him into losing his temper, tried to shoo him out of the kitchen. "Why don't you go up to your room, dear, and make a start on your homework? Then you can have the evening free to do what you like. Your tea won't be ready for at least an hour."

"I don't want to start on my homework!"

She sighed. "Just keep out from under my feet, that's all! I've got so much on my mind I don't know whether I'm coming or going! And, talking of feet, take off your shoes. I don't want mud on the carpets."

"Mud! It hasn't rained for days!"

"Take them off, all the same."

"Why are you all dressed up like that?" She looked very smart in a navy-blue outfit; her mouth was properly lipsticked and she was wearing her pearl ear-rings. She had obviously found time to visit the hairdresser too. Colin often felt that when Mum took the trouble she could make herself exceedingly pretty; she was the sort of mother you were pleased to have at those boring school functions that parents always came

6

to, like open day or the end-of-term concert. He wondered what Wootton's mother looked like, assuming she existed at all: some fly-blown hag, he supposed, soaked in gin, with bloated purplish legs and varicose veins. The idea pleased him, and he felt more cheerful.

"Colin, you have a brain like a sieve!" Mrs Lockwood exclaimed, and she glowered at June, who had started tittering again. "Think, will you?"

"I can't."

"Shop. Fashion show. Remember?"

"Oh yes." How could he forget! His mother was the assistant manageress of Nimrod's, the expensive dress shop in the High Street, and this evening there was to be a fashion show, the new lines for next autumn. With the war on there would, of course, be no mannequin parade, no bizarre girls in outlandish creations; instead, there was a film, in colour. The new clothes would not be very exotic, just last year's old things with a bit of trimming here and there to make them look as if they were new. Colin had never been to one of these sessions – wild horses wouldn't drag him into a stronghold so feminine, so filled with contralto voices and heaving bosoms, perfumes and silk stockings – but Mrs Lockwood had been rattling on so much recently about tonight's "do" that he felt as if he knew more about it than did any of the shop assistants who worked under her eagle eye. There was some important person coming to show the film, someone who was travelling down from London specially, from the head office in Kensington: he tried to remember her name; it was as preposterous as his mother's description of her character. What was it? If he could say it aloud June would explode with giggles; Mum would get angry with her, and . . . and what? He wasn't quite sure why he wanted his mother to be annoyed with June, but he felt it might give him some satisfaction. Some sympathy, perhaps.

"Lorna Wimbleball," he said.

June choked in her cup, and Pamela, who was eating bread and raspberry jam, put both hands to her mouth to stop the food flying out on to the table.

"Now then!" Mrs Lockwood said, threateningly. But once the process had started it was impossible to stop. Both girls shook from head to toe; their faces went bright red; their eyes bulged and tears brimmed.

"Wimbleball!" June spluttered.

Pamela could contain herself no longer. Bits of half-chewed bread and jam shot out of her mouth as the laugh burst from her; one flew up over June's head in a neat curve and landed on the draining-board. Mrs Lockwood knew it was ill-mannered to shout at a guest; she was aware, in any case, that it was not altogether the fault of either of the girls, so she vented all her anger on Colin.

"You said that quite deliberately, Colin!"

"I did not."

"Quite deliberately! You knew perfectly well that these two would have hysterics the moment you mentioned that name. I'm sick and tired of this nonsense, sick and tired of it! Get out of this room at once. Go on! Get out!"

"But—"

"GET OUT!!"

He took refuge in the lounge, thinking there might be something on the wireless in which he could immerse himself, but he was out of luck there too. Mary and her boy-friend were in residence; they were listening to a gramophone record of "Swan Lake", expressions of romantic nonsense written all over their moony faces.

Mary turned on him frostily. "Be quiet," she said.

8

"I haven't said a word. Now, honestly, have I? Not one word."

"You have now. You're spoiling the *pas de deux*."

"Oh *pas de deux*! Pardon me!" He flung his arms in the air and kicked up one leg in imitation of a ballet-dancer. The vibration caused the needle to jump back a groove; Mary stood up angrily and turned the record off.

"If that's scratched, I'll kill you," she said. "I paid good money for that, and I don't see why a little squirt like you should come in here and ruin it!"

"Mary, why don't you just shut up?"

"Why don't you go into the other room and leave us alone?"

He sat down in an armchair and glared at her.

"Play it again," said the boy-friend. "Play it again. It may not be harmed."

She did so, and they all three listened in silence, or, rather, Mary and her young man listened; the music flowed over Colin like so much extraneous noise. He tried to work out exactly why he disliked his elder sister so much. She was fearsomely ugly, of course; her nose was far too big, and her hair was mousy and always untidy. And she was fat: she certainly hadn't inherited their mother's neat figure and good looks. But these were not very convincing reasons for disliking her. Once they had been good friends, but now that she was eighteen, nearly grown up, she seemed to have little time for him. She was training to be a nurse, and when she was off duty there was usually a boy-friend in tow. Colin wondered for a moment if he was jealous in some way, but he could not understand why he should be, and dismissed the idea as ridiculous. The current boy-friend had, in any case, lasted longer than any of the others; the family had grown used to him. Lars was half-English and half-Swedish, a tall, gangling blond; his ambition was to be a dancer,

9

but his call-up papers had arrived. He would be off in three days' time. Since Mary had met him she had taken an instant passionate interest in ballet, a subject she had not previously shown any concern for at all. Their mother approved. Mrs Lockwood recalled visits to Sadlers Wells years ago, and her own adolescent dreams of dancing on the stage; tea-time conversation often revolved these days round names like Pavlova, Diaghilev, and Nijinsky. Colin felt at a great disadvantage, and thought, in any case, that there must be something queer about a man wanting to be a ballet-dancer, though his feelings changed one evening after he had seen Lars playing tennis with a friend: he hit the ball with speed, strength, indeed brilliance.

Lars stretched out on the sofa and gazed up at the ceiling, while the Tchaikovsky music filled the room. He was completely absorbed; Mary on the other hand sat tense and upright on her chair, watching him through half-closed eyes. Colin had once asked Mary why someone who was half-Swedish should be in Exeter, of all places, in 1942; why could he not claim immunity from call-up, for Sweden was a neutral country, surely? Maybe Lars was a spy, he suggested. Mary poured scorn on the idea; it was a typical example of her brother's half-witted mentality. Why wasn't he interned then, or why wasn't his father (who was a native of Stockholm) sent back to Sweden? The Swedes might be neutral, but they weren't exactly popular, were they? They had allowed Hitler to send his troops through their country to attack Norway, or so it was rumoured. They hadn't lifted a finger to help Finland, either, when that country had been attacked by Russia in the winter war of 1939. Mary said Colin had got all his facts wrong as usual; the Swedes had not allowed German troops through, and Finland was an ally of Nazi Germany. As for Lars's father, he was a naturalised British citizen, had lived in England for years, and was some important person in the Exeter telephone exchange. Colin had no right to be so nosy; it wasn't any of his business.

The record finished. "One day, Mary," Lars said, "I will dance this for you."

"Oh, Lars! Will you really?"

"Just for you." He held out his hand and touched hers.

Lovers, Colin thought, disgustedly, they never had time for anyone but themselves. Now that Lars was looking into her eyes Mary seemed to have forgotten that there was a slight click on the record where the needle had jumped. Colin felt completely unwanted, and in his own home too! He hadn't the slightest intention of starting his homework till after he had eaten, and as for that stupid essay, he'd have to invent some brilliant excuse for not doing it. A vulture swooped down and snatched it out of my hand as I was crossing the road. It had been run over by a bus. My father accidentally took it to work, thinking it was some precious manuscript from the cathedral library, and gave it to the Bishop. No. I left it on your desk before school started, sir; haven't you found it? Something like that perhaps. Whatever happened he was definitely *not* going to write it!

He stood up, left the room, and walked out of the house. A stroll into town, perhaps to the cathedral to chat with Dad, would do him good, he thought.

Although most of the bombs of the previous night had fallen on Wonford and Pennsylvania, some had been scattered at random on other parts of the city. In Barnfield Road one house which had received a direct hit was now a pile of shattered masonry, glass and wood. Colin stared at it, amazed and horrified. He did not know who the occupants were, but it was a house he had often walked past, being only a few hundred yards

II

from where he lived himself, in Denmark Road. An old Victorian building it had been, set well back in its garden, with two gates and a curving drive that had been intended perhaps as the way in and way out for horse-drawn carriages. There had been ivy on its walls and dark blue curtains in the windows; he remembered once, when he was a little kid, telling his mother that that was the place he was going to live in when he grew up, and she had said she hoped he'd be able to afford it, because neither she nor his father would ever see the inside of such a palatial mansion. Palatial, what was that? A palace, she answered, like where the king lived.

Now there was a huge hole in the ground where the bomb had exploded, and the rubble that had been the house was a gigantic heap, rather like a huge bonfire prepared for Guy Fawkes' night. The flowers in the garden continued to bloom as if nothing had happened: tulips, aubretia and alyssum in neat beds; sweet-scented purple lilac against the fence, and laburnums by the gates, their long pendants of dazzling yellow hanging like so many burning lanterns.

His first feeling on entering the door at the west end of the cathedral was fright: if a bomb fell this instant on the nave roof, all these stone trees that were the pillars supporting the vault, the galleries, the stained-glass windows, would cave in, would collapse on to his head, mutilating him, severing his limbs from his body, burying him fathoms deep under a mountain of broken stone. That was silly: the air-raid warning had not sounded, and, if it did, there was plenty of time to get out and find a shelter, and, anyway, Exeter had hardly ever suffered an attack in daylight. Yet. Suppose the mechanism of the air-raid warning system failed to work? Or the Germans had found a way of silencing it?

He made himself concentrate instead on a tablet on the wall, a memorial to a nineteenth-century general. Of course, of course, of course! Why hadn't he thought of it before? This was the very thing needed to impress old Kitchen! It had been carved by an ancestor on Mum's side of the family, her great-great-something-grandfather. Sanders was her maiden name. Brenda Sanders, who had taken for her lawful wedded husband Ronald Lockwood. There was the name, very tiny, in the bottom right-hand corner: Paul Sanders, mason. Mum knew nothing about him, where he had lived or who he had married, only that there was a brother who had emigrated to America and grown very rich: there were descendants, cousins hundreds of times removed, in Louisville or Los Angeles or somewhere, that her family had lost touch with half a century ago. Colin read the inscription carefully, then hunted in his pocket for a pencil and, not finding one, decided to search on the bookstall at the far end of the nave. He looked round. There was nobody about. He picked up a pamphlet entitled "The Truth about the Church of England" which had a blank page inside its cover, and found a pencil in the drawer of the table on which the postcards and guide-books were displayed. He hurried back to the memorial and copied out the inscription.

SACRED TO THE MEMORY OF

HORATIO JAMES HERBERT

LIEUTENANT GENERAL IN THE ARMY

AND COLONEL OF THE 19TH REGIMENT OF FOOT

WHO DIED ON THE 4TH DAY OF JULY 1848

AGED 61

IN WHOSE LIFE AND CHARACTER THE VIRTUES OF THE HERO, THE
PATRIOT AND THE CHRISTIAN, WERE SO EMINENTLY CONSPICUOUS
THAT IT MAY JUSTLY BE SAID HE SERVED THE QUEEN AND HER

COUNTRY WITH A ZEAL EXCEEDED ONLY BY HIS PIETY TOWARDS
HIS GOD.

Paul Sanders, mason

Excellent! That was his history homework done!

Footsteps. His father was coming towards him. "Locking-up time," Dad said. "Visiting hours are over and the choir's just about to start a practice. I'm going up the south tower. Do you want to come with me?"

Colin smiled with real pleasure, for the first time that day. "You bet! Thanks, Dad."

"Don't tell the Dean, whatever you do."

The twin towers of the cathedral, the most ancient part of the fabric, had been closed to visitors since the beginning of the war. The Dean and chapter had decided that if there was an air-raid it would be impossible to fetch people down in time, and there might be accidents on the narrow spiral staircases if some-body panicked. Only the vergers were allowed up there now, and the small band of fire-watchers who stayed every night on the top of each tower: their duty was to deal with incendiary bombs on the cathedral roof, to take all measures possible to ex-tinguish fires before any damage was done. So far they had had a very dull war; not one incendiary had touched the cathedral.

Colin followed his father. The choir started to sing: "Have mercy upon me, O God, according to thy lovingkindness: according unto the multitude of Thy tender mercies blot out my transgressions".

"The Miserere by Allegri," said Mr Lockwood.

"I thought allegri meant fast in music."

"Allegro. Why was I blessed with ignorant uncultured children?"

"Don't know, Dad. A punishment for *your* transgressions,

14

maybe."

"Ssh! Listen!"

They stood still. The music was not loud but it seemed to fill the entire building, stroking echoes and rustling whispers out of the arches and pillars, making the stone almost melt or float, and when a boy treble hit an almost impossibly high C Colin thought the cathedral must surely lift a little from the ground to accommodate it or else its vault would crack. He looked up: it was all still solidly there. It was not music that moved him (though of course it sent Dad into ecstasies) but, yes, the quality of the singing was, he had to admit, as perfect as the cathedral itself.

Inside the spiral staircase the choir was suddenly cut off. Colin felt his knees weakening slowly from the effort of climbing so many steps, but at last they were walking on level ground, along the middle of what appeared to be a vast triangular-shaped tunnel of semi-darkness. "The top of the nave vaulting," Dad explained. "Don't step off this cat-walk; the stone is thin and I don't want you crashing through to the floor below. Apart from which Bishop Grandisson's tracery hasn't been tampered with since thirteen-something and it would cost rather a lot to repair."

Above their heads were the timbers supporting the lead roof of the cathedral, ancient and huge, like ships' masts. It was musty and airless in this tunnel; cobwebs brushed their faces: the silence, broken only by far-off fragments of music and their own footsteps, was thick and muffling, like an eiderdown.

"Why have you come up here, Dad?" Colin asked.

"To check the buckets and stirrup-pumps, see if there's enough sand and water. I don't trust these fire-watchers. Students! St Luke's students too; they're even less reliable than the ones from the University! I'm told they spend most of their time running races up and down the towers. Must be a bit boring, I suppose, keeping an eye open for fires that never happen, but if there was a blaze and nothing to put it out with, the Dean might ask some rather awkward questions."

He opened a door and they entered the room from which, before the war, the bells were rung; this was in the tower itself, about half-way up. There was a sand-bin in one corner, stirrup-pumps in another, and a line of buckets suspended from the hooks on which the bell-ringers used to hang their jackets.

"Go on up if you want," Dad said. "I'll be busy in here for a while. I'm too old to climb stairs I don't need to."

"Is it far?"

"You'll find out." He grinned. "I'll wait here for you. Go through that door there."

Colin climbed up. He found himself in a little room which was littered with pieces of metal twisted into strange shapes; here a man used to work every day repairing the lead sheets and fleur-de-lys decorations of the cathedral roof. But no-one had been employed here since the beginning of the war. Everything was shrouded in dust. There was a small furnace, centuries old, rusty with disuse. A tin mug lay on its side on the floor; the last lead-maker had probably drunk from it during his tea-break on September 2nd, 1939.

More stairs. It was hot; he took off his jacket. Now he was in the bell-chamber itself. Sinister and huge the bells seemed in the half-light: he could just make out the names of some of them, Grandisson, Purdue, Pennington, Pongamouth, Doom. Doom! Would it ring on the day of judgement, warn of some terrible air-raid that would devastate the city utterly? He kicked it with his foot, and listened to the faint deep bong die into silence. Wood creaked. If the tower should ever be hit all these bells would crash down with the masonry on to the floor

16

of the transept below in a raucous jangling clanging caco-
phony, blasting ear-drums like in "The Nine Tailors"; the
sound of doomsday.

He emerged into daylight to find the top of the tower surpris-
ingly small: a squat pyramid of lead, around which it was possible to walk easily enough, and on the other side of him the
familiar castellated battlements that he usually saw from below
or glimpsed at a distance between the buildings of the city.
Underfoot, pigeon-droppings in great quantities. The north
tower, with its single bell, Great Peter, one of the largest bells in
the world, blocked the view ahead, but on either side the city
stretched out for him to inspect: the bishop's palace, his school,
St Luke's College, houses, shops, churches, trees – he was surprised at the great number of trees – the river, the long ridge of
Haldon on the south-west sky-line, the estuary, the sea. The city
was contained entirely within the rim of its hills; for the first
time ever he had a sense of it as a whole, could see the plan of the
medieval builders, the line of the ancient walls, how in the last
century it had burst through these walls as more and more
houses were needed for its growing population. Here he was on
the summit of its highest and oldest building: king of his own
city. No-one in Exeter at that moment was as tall as he was,
could see it as he did.

He remembered Mr Kitchen's hackneyed phrase: "Every
stone has a tale to tell." And he began to realise that the old
fool's way of teaching history was, after all, rather more inter-
esting than memorising dates of battles and Acts of Parliament.

When he was walking home with his father he remembered
that he had left his jacket on the roof of the tower.

"You'll lose your head one day," Dad said.

"My history homework is in one of the pockets. And my

money, and my wallet, and –"

"I'm going back later. I'll get one of the students to fetch it down."

"You're sure it's all right? It might blow over the edge!"

"There's not a breath of wind this evening. Nor a cloud in the sky, either." Dad looked up towards Haldon. "Full moon to-night, so we may have a raid. Your jacket couldn't blow away in weather like this and I don't think it's a target Hitler's particularly interested in."

Two

Mrs Lockwood put the phone down and said to Mary "That is the last straw! What on earth am I going to do? I'm expecting about fifty women at this film show; there's sherry and things on sticks to be served to them and no-one to do it!"

"Why, what's happened?"

"Mrs Blackie's son has broken three ribs falling off a bus, if you please! He's supposed to be supervising all the refreshments, and now he's in hospital. *Such* a nice young man, too! He always makes a good impression on the customers and they have an extra drink just because he's pouring it out. Then they feel in a good mood and buy all sorts of clothes they wouldn't dream of paying for if they were stone cold sober!"

"Sounds very immoral. Look, Mum, don't flap. Lars and I will do it."

"But you're going to the pictures." She looked anxiously in the mirror, and pushed a few stray hairs back into place. Her neck was a little pink: she must not come up in a hot flush tonight, she must not: it made her look so tense, so old.

"It doesn't matter," said Mary. "We can go another time."

"But you can't. This is your only night off, isn't it? And whatever would Lars say! All those women gabbling about dresses and hats! It's hardly his cup of tea, is it? Lady Crediton will be there, and you know what *she's* like when there's a handsome young man around!"

"Sometimes, Mum, I think you fancy Lars yourself."

"Mary, you do talk the most utter nonsense! Anyway, I wouldn't dream of spoiling your evening. You go to the film. Dad and I saw it the night before last; it's really romantic! Deanna Durbin!" She went all starry-eyed for a moment, lost in the memory of "It started with Eve", then glanced again in the mirror. "How do I look? Enough lipstick? Or too much?"

"Fine. But what are you going to do about the booze?"

"Only one thing I can do. Ask Colin."

"Colin!! Mum, are you absolutely off your head? Can you imagine Colin pouring out sherry and making polite conversation to Lady Crediton? He'll turn bright red and stutter and spill sherry all over the place, or swig from the bottle when he thinks no-one's looking and get tipsy, and when Mrs Wimbleball launches into negligées and super little outfits to wear at race meetings or cocktail parties he'll go berserk laughing!"

"No he won't. I shall bribe him."

"Bribe him!"

"Yes. I'll offer him ten shillings if he'll do it *and* promise to behave himself."

"I should make it a pound if I were you."

"Maybe you're right. A pound. Out of the till. I'll put it down to expenses." She went into the kitchen, and took a shepherd's pie out of the oven. Colin could do it, she thought. Sometimes he could be quite well-mannered. Sometimes. And he would soon be just as handsome as Bob Blackie, tall for his age, dark-haired: he had Ron's blue eyes and wide smiling mouth. In a year or two girls would be flocking round him; she hoped he'd know what was what, how to manage. "Where is he, anyway? And your father? Their supper's ready, and, as usual, they're not here."

Mary looked out of the window. "They're just coming up the garden. They're peering at the vegetables. Dad's prodding at those turnips or parsnips or whatever they are. Colin's doing gymnastics on a branch of the cherry tree."

"I didn't ask for a running commentary! It's not the St Leger. And don't you know the difference between a turnip and a parsnip?"

"No."

"Honestly, Mary, whatever did they teach you at that school?" She dished out shepherd's pie and cabbage on to five plates. "Tell Lars to come and eat. And put some knives and forks on the table. And *don't* say a word to Colin when I ask him about this evening. One joke, one rude word from you or Lars and he'll refuse. And when your father's upstairs washing his hands, tell him to be quiet about it too. Where's June?"

"Playing round at Pamela's house."

"Thank Heaven for that. One enemy out of the way at least."

Colin's first reaction was one of such shock and horror that he dropped his knife on the floor, then stared at his mother, mouth open and speechless. He looked suspiciously at the others, but Dad went on eating, quite unconcerned, almost as if he hadn't heard, and Lars and Mary continued with their conversation: Marshal Timoshenko's forces, Lars said, had cut the railway between Moscow and Kharkov; it was in this evening's Express and Echo and it was a further sign that Hitler's invasion of Russia was the mistake that would ultimately lose him the war. Mary nodded. Silly twerp, Colin thought: Lars could say anything, true, false, childish or outrageous, and Mary would go on nodding in that same dumb, cow-like way.

"Conservatives will win the by-election in Putney on Thursday," Dad said. "Vastly reduced majority is my prediction."

Mrs Lockwood frowned at everybody, then returned to the attack. It wasn't every day a boy of nearly fifteen was presented with a lot of money for doing almost next to nothing. All he had to do was wash himself *properly*, put on his suit, and Colin did look nice in his suit; she was always proud to be seen with him when he took the trouble to smarten himself up. There was no need for him to talk to anybody if he didn't feel like it, just pour out drinks and go round with plates of cheese biscuits and celery and sausages and offer them to people — such a pity the firm couldn't provide anything more elaborate, but, being wartime, they were lucky to get even sausages — and when the fashion show started he didn't have to stay, he could just collect up the dirty glasses and wash them for her, have a drink himself if there was anything left, then slip out and come home. Silence. Colin filled his mouth with cabbage and thought about it. A pound was certainly unexpected. He would then have enough money to buy the new fishing-rod he was after. The only trouble was Kitchen's essay. He had decided he would have to do it after all; none of the excuses he had thought of, joking or serious, would possibly suffice.

"I've got an essay to write," he said. "On four sides of foolscap."

"Don't talk with your mouth full," his mother said. "Can't it wait?"

"No."

"What's it about?"

"Er . . . I'd rather not say."

"Why? Is it a punishment?"

"Er . . . Yes. I fell asleep in the History lesson."

"I'm not surprised after last night! Don't your teachers know there's a war on?"

"Kitchen certainly does. He's having a private war. Against me. And at the moment he's winning."

"Ah, he'll lose in the end," said Dad. "Napoleon did." He picked up the newspaper and started to read.

"What's the essay about?" Mrs Lockwood asked.

"If you really must know, its title is 'Why I am a fool'."

Mary shrieked with laughter, Lars looked bewildered, and Dad hurriedly read aloud from the paper: "It says here that housewives are asked to use non-rationed foods as much as possible, particularly meats such as ox's or pig's liver, kidneys, tripe and sheep's hearts, which can make inexpensive yet fully nourishing dishes. And . . . men in the Forces, who are most appreciative of the knitted comforts sent them, need more socks. The colours wanted are Navy and Air Force blue, grey and khaki, in sizes eight to eleven. And please knit with adequate leg-length — some of the socks coming in are far too short in the foot and leg. Well, Mary, there's a job for you."

"Ron, will you stop being so stupid!" Mrs Lockwood said, in an exasperated tone of voice. Dad looked at her with mild astonishment, and passed the paper to Mary. "Well, Colin, fool you may be or not," she went on, "but I'll join you against the Kitchen front. I'll write him a note and explain why you can't do it."

"Why . . . thanks, Mum!" Colin was delighted. "Of course I'll pour your sherry. I'd love to. What will you say, to Mr Kitchen, I mean?"

"Hmmm . . . that you wrote it and I accidentally burned it or put it in the dustbin, or something."

"Do you think that's wise?" Dad asked.

"Why not?"

"Suppose Mrs Kitchen turns up at your party at Nimrod's? Or even the man himself?"

"Impossible," Colin said. "He's at least a hundred and nine, so she must be an old witch with a moustache. Probably bedridden and toothless. People like that don't shop at Nimrod's. Anyway, I don't know if there is a Mrs Kitchen. I can't imagine anyone being married to him, unless she's blind or stark staring bonkers. Or shuts her eyes in bed and thinks of Clark Gable."

"Colin, that's no way to talk," Mum said, severely.

"Well," said Dad, "I'm going to do a spot of gardening while the weather's so good. And if you and your mother run into trouble I don't know anything about your essay and I've never heard of Mr Kitchen. It's nothing to do with me. Anyway . . . enjoy yourselves, all of you. Don't keep Mary out too late, Lars."

"I won't."

"And Colin . . . don't drink too much!"

Dig for victory, thought Mr Lockwood, as he turned over a spadeful of earth. The only pleasure this war had brought so far was that he had been able to double the extent of his vegetable patch. His wife had, years ago, filled the garden with useless things like flowers: he had to admit that they looked pretty, particularly now, in the spring, when shrubs like kerria and flowering currant were in bloom, and the bulbs, and lupins and irises, but what use were they? A garden ought to be productive; there was nothing so satisfying as tasting your own peas and beans and sprouts picked an hour before from your own piece of earth. Two years ago, in answer to the government's call for people to grow as much of their own food as they possibly could, he had dug up most of the flowerbeds, despite his wife's protests, and planted them with potatoes, cauliflowers

24

and cabbages.

It wasn't often he could find a spare evening, however, to devote to his hobby. Since the war had started he had never worked so hard in his life. The two youngest vergers had been called up and not replaced, which meant the day-to-day running of the cathedral fell entirely on himself and Mr Alderdyce, the second verger, who was so old and forgetful that many of his duties had to be carried out by Mr Lockwood himself. Fortunately the Dean had agreed to the idea of curtailing visiting hours to a brief period in the morning and two hours late in the afternoon, but all the services had to be attended to, and choir practices, music recitals and chapter meetings organised. There was also the problem of what might happen in an air-raid. The fire-watchers were inefficient, and there were priceless treasures in the cathedral which would not be easy to rescue if a really big fire took hold. The medieval glass, admittedly, had been taken out of the east window, and the Bishop's throne, a massive piece of oak, carved in the thirteenth century, had been dismantled and stored in a cellar, but there were mitres, copes, chasubles, the altar plate, ancient wooden chests, the Elizabethan lectern, candlesticks that dated from Charles the Second's time, and many other objects of inestimable worth still in the cathedral and in use. It was a continual worry, and what to do about it was a continual source of friction between himself and the Dean.

Even now, while he was thinking of the vegetables he would be able to eat later in the summer, and seeing in his mind's eye the clusters of fat pea-pods, the feathery tops of carrots, the rows of bean-poles, it was difficult not to forget the problems of altar-cloths and chalices. The flag Captain Scott had taken to the South Pole was still hanging from the wall of the nave; it was unique, irreplaceable, and the Dean had insisted it should not be removed!

June came into the garden, absent-mindedly bouncing a ball on a tennis racket. "One potato, two potato, three potato, four," she sang. "Five potato, six potato, seven potato – "

"Nine in fact," said Dad, looking at his watch. "It's time you were in bed."

"Can't I wait till Mum comes home?"

"Certainly not. She's going to the pub with all her girls after the fashion show, so Heaven alone knows how long she'll be." He stooped, picked up some weeds and chucked them on to the compost heap.

"Half an hour, then?"

"All right. Half an hour. But don't tell your mother."

"Dad . . . are we ever going to be able to use the car again?" She dropped the tennis racket, and threw the ball from one hand to the other.

"Not till the war's over, child."

"The weather's so warm. I'd love to swim in the sea again. Pam says you can swim up on the north coast, near Hartland Quay. Her dad's taking her up there next weekend."

"Where does he find the petrol coupons? Black market, I suppose."

"I don't know." She bounced her tennis-ball against the fence, a rather wistful expression on her face. Mr Lockwood felt a sudden stab of anger: why shouldn't his daughter be allowed all the normal pleasures of childhood, days on the beach, nice clothes to wear, fruit like bananas and melons, proper fresh eggs, cream, untroubled nights of sleep? He hoped Hitler would burn in Hell! Poor kid, with her sweet innocent face and pigtails: she might not yet understand all the implications of what Rommel or Timoshenko were doing on their various fronts, might not even wonder what would happen next if the Nazis did defeat Russia, but last night's air-raid had terrified her out of her wits, much more than it had the rest of the family. Colin, for instance, seemed to think it was all a great lark. A wartime childhood, he thought, wasn't perhaps horrifying; it wouldn't necessarily scar you for life: but it was dull and shabby, often boring, a constant succession of deprivations, thou shalt nots.

"I'll ask Pam's father if he'll take you," he said. "You deserve a treat."

"Will you?" Her face brightened. "But . . . should you? Ask, I mean? They might think it's rude."

"He owes me a favour."

"What for?"

"I got him front row seats for the Grandisson service last Christmas Eve. They were supposed to be reserved for the Archdeacon of Barnstaple's mother-in-law and her friend. Two dear old ladies they are; I verged them hurriedly into the north transept, saying they'd hear better. As they're both quite deaf it made no odds."

June smiled. "You're as bad as Mum."

"What do you mean?" She looked just like her mother when she smiled, he thought. Same dimples and dancing eyes. Same shape to her hair, too.

"Giving Colin a pound for pouring out drinks! I'd have done it for ten bob."

He laughed. "You're all completely mercenary in this family! Apart from Mary. She *volunteered* to do it. Free, I think."

"Mary's a nut-case. She's gone quite soppy and spoony over that ballet-dancer. I don't like him. He sucks up to Mum all the time, and Mum says he's ever so polite and that, but I can see he's only trying to make a good impression."

"What's wrong with trying to make a good impression?"

27

"Nothing, I suppose." She bent down, and pulled some clover out of the flower-bed. "But . . . he's wet, Lars. Well, I think so."

"How did you know Mum offered Colin a pound?"

"He told me." She tore the leaves off the clover. "Dad . . . do you think Lars and Mary will get married?"

He stared at her, amazed. The idea had never, previously, occurred to him. "That is not the sort of question, young lady, to which I know the answer," he said. "However, I think it's high time we went indoors. And before you go upstairs you can make me a nice cup of tea." He collected up his gardening tools, put them in the shed, and they both slowly made their way back to the house.

"I miss the street lamps," Lars said. "What's the famous saying? 'The lights are going out all over Europe. They will not come on again in our time'."

"We used to have lights on our Christmas tree," Mary said. "All the colours of the rainbow. But they fused the year before last, and you can't get replacements. Not an essential industry, like tanks."

"You sound bitter."

"No."

"Sad then."

"Perhaps. You leave the day after tomorrow." They were strolling up the High Street, hand in hand, gazing into shop windows. They were early for the film. However, there was little of interest: just ugly clothes, ugly furniture. Shopkeepers had great difficulty these days in filling up the space in their windows; everything looked run-down and shoddy. Though the air-raids had so far missed the High Street almost completely, there were a few cracked panes of glass, or letters missing from shop signs: . LEXAN . . . . LEAN . . . was all that remained of Alexandra Cleaners. And, anyway, it was almost impossible to judge whether the goods displayed were worth the prices or the number of coupons demanded; the glass fronts were sometimes so thickly plastered with transparent sticky tape that the effect was like looking into a water-filled tank: Mary half-expected tropical fish or mermaids to float between the dress-makers' dummies.

A man and a woman with three young children walked past; they were all weighed down with bulky luggage: the man carried a mattress, his wife a bundle of sheets and blankets, and the children each clutched a pillow and a few ragged toys.

"Bombed out, I suppose," Lars said.

An old woman came towards them wheeling bedclothes on a handcart; beyond her and all down the street people struggled with mattresses, sleeping-bags and other articles of bedding.

"Whatever's happening?" Mary wondered.

"I don't know. Look, there's a policeman stopping that family. What's he doing?"

"Persuaded them to turn back, it looks like. Some sort of unofficial evacuation? The sirens haven't gone." She looked up, anxiously. No sign of enemy planes: just a big empty sky. A warm spring evening. "I know what it is," she said. "It's because of last night's air-raid."

"What do you mean?"

"You know. After the raids last month lots of people wouldn't sleep at home. Don't you remember? They trekked out to the fields beyond Whipton and Heavitree. Terrified of being killed by their own houses collapsing on top of them, but the police say the bombs fall anywhere so they could just as easily be killed in the open as indoors. And all that time wasted digging in the rubble looking for people trapped and buried alive when there may not be anybody underneath at all!"

How Mary loved to impart information he already knew, Lars thought. Detail after detail! "They think there'll be another raid tonight, then?" he said.

"The sky's very clear, isn't it? It's possible."

He put his arm round her. "Come on. We don't want to be late." They walked on in silence. Mary felt depressed. In two days' time Lars would be leaning out of a train window at St David's Station: good-bye, good-bye! Where was he going? Would he ever come back? Like thousands of other farewells at war-time stations, men in uniforms, waving; girls on the platforms, brave smiles and handkerchiefs. We'll meet again, don't know where, don't know when. Like on the films. Like real life.

Did he love her? He hadn't said. Marry her and have children when he returned from the war, fulfill his ambition to be a dancer? The questions were absurd. In a month or two he could be dead. Many young people, impelled by that knowledge, had rushed into declarations of love, hurried to the altar in these war years and might possibly live to regret it: relationships should grow like trees, slow and solid, not bloom like desert flowers. The metaphors came, she recalled, from a women's magazine story. Recently she had been reading more and more serials in women's magazines; they filled her few spare moments at the hospital or at home, prevented her from being unhappy. But they got in the way when she tried to think about her feelings for Lars: they stopped her being completely herself, and made her romanticise him, absurdly.

But she loved him. She was sure of that. She would say 'yes'.

"There's a queue," he said.

It shuffled forward slowly. The cinema was crowded, more than they had expected, but soon they were inside in the warm

comfortable dark, adjusting their eyes to the huge nearness of
the figures on the screen. It was worrying that they weren't at
the back, by a gangway: if there was an air-raid, and they had to
run out and find shelter, it would be much easier if they were
close to the exit. There had been nasty stories about people
being killed in cinemas that had had direct hits.

Lars nuzzled his face against hers.

The newsreel finished, then the advertisements. The lights
came on. They looked round, trying to recognise friends. The
doors at the back were not shut; people were still coming in.
Cigarette smoke. It was much quieter without the film voices,
the film music. Just the hum of ordinary conversation.

Faintly, as if from a great distance, there came through the
open doors the thin whine of the air-raid warning.

Three

THE ATTENDANCE at Nimrod's autumn fashion show was disappointingly small; the previous night's air-raid had decided many of the usual customers not to venture out. Colin acquitted himself quite reasonably, Mrs Lockwood thought; he was most helpful with the plates of biscuits and sausages, and made sure that when a glass was almost empty a re-fill was offered. He was rather stiff and poker-faced, perhaps, like a nervous butler, not the relaxed charmer Bob Blackie was, but no matter; he was only fourteen, after all. Lady Crediton asked who the young man was; "Oh, your *son!*" she exclaimed when Mrs Lockwood told her. "My dear, he does you *immense* credit!" Colin scowled at her. "So many young men these days have no manners. No manners at all! The wrong sort of people are creeping in *everywhere!*" Colin wondered what her son was like. Some effete freak, no doubt, chinless and emasculated.

"Glad to see you can do something well, Lockwood," a man's voice said behind him. Colin turned. It was Mr Kitchen.

"S-s-sweet or dry, sir?" he stammered.

"Dry for me, please, and sweet for Mrs Kitchen."

Colin retired to the little improvised bar and poured the drinks out with a shaking hand. He had noticed that it was not completely unheard of for a man to come to this sort of occasion; sprinkled among the thirty or so ladies present were half a dozen husbands, dragged along, he assumed, by domineering wives they couldn't say no to. But Mr Kitchen, of all people! His wife, too, was an astonishment: youngish, well-dressed, almost good-looking!

"So your mother is one of the staff?" Mr Kitchen asked, evidently wanting to stop and make polite conversation. "I didn't know that. Has she worked here long?"

"Several years, sir. Excuse me, sir, I have to . . . er . . ."

He escaped, and, needing to steady his nerves, swallowed a whole sherry in one mouthful. There was a shout for quiet, then the voice of Miss Garland, the manageress, requesting people to come through to the inner room of the shop, for Mrs Wimbleball was ready to start. Colin was very relieved to see Mr and Mrs Kitchen among the first to go in. When everyone had drifted away, he began to collect up the empty glasses, thinking that the whole experience, except for the arrival of the Kitchens, had been quite entertaining; what a mixed crowd of people the Nimrod customers were! Some had affected voices, acres of make-up and oceans of scent, but others were just ordinary; Mrs Overton, who kept the sweet-shop opposite his school, was there, not in her usual pinafore of course, but dressed up in her glad rags so that she was almost unrecognizable. And he had exchanged a few words with Mrs Hill, the fat old farmer's wife from Exwick, who used to sell eggs to his family before the war started.

His mother came up and gripped his arm. "Thanks, Colin. You did splendidly." She was tense and excited, flushed round the neck, he noticed. "I can't stop. There was something wrong with the film projector, but I think it's all right now."

What was Mrs Wimbleball like, he wondered. If she was as

grotesque as some of the Nimrod customers, it would be a pity not to go in and listen. He could wash up later, he supposed; it wouldn't matter. If he could creep in at the back, unobserved, and stay for a few minutes . . .

There was an empty chair just inside the doorway, next to his mother. She stared at him, somewhat surprised, but said nothing.

Lorna Wimbleball was very tall and thin, with cropped grey hair; she did not wear the mass of jewellery sported by most of the customers: in fact she looked quite plain and ordinary, with a pair of spectacles that dangled from a chain round her neck. Colin's first impression was that she would prove, from his point of view, to be poor quality amusement, but as soon as she opened her mouth, he realised she would exceed all his expectations.

"I've had electricians *haring* in from the whole of Exeter all afternoon" – sweeping hand gestures in every direction – "just to peep at this little machine. It's so old, poor thing, and needs *so* many new parts I just can't count them all up! Anyway, a dear little man Brenda found for me spent *ages* welding it and it's going like magic!" She rapped the top of the projector with a cane. "Off we go, Daphne darling." A picture of a tall willowy female, a sort of younger version of Mrs Wimbleball herself, came into view on the screen; she was leaning sideways in an uncomfortable pose and was draped in a large number of long-looking garments. "Isn't that nice? Isn't it?" There were murmurs of agreement from several customers. "That's one of our colours for this autumn, a rather gorgeous shade of crushed *blackberry*. And very few coupons needed. We call it the 'Dietrich look', the costume co-ordinated with the long scarf and matching hat. Co-ordination. That's what I want to emphasise, ladies. We at Nimrod know that with a war on you can't just

34

simply *throw* away all last year's clothes into the dustbin! Build on what you've already got; that's our motto. Co-ordination." The same young woman came into view, this time in a floral dress. "Isn't that nice? Isn't it?" More murmurs of agreement, not quite so vigorous as last time. "You can wear this for simply *anything*. Throw it in a carrier bag and when some *super* man rings you up at the office and says, darling, I'm sure you've had a ghastly day, do come out for a drink, you can just *throw* it on and look totally stunning! Notice the long pleats of the skirt; we call it the 'Tube Line', and you can buy it in the blackberry, or tangerine, or my favourite, a sort of delicate pale watery greengage."

Colin's first reaction was one of amazed disbelief: it couldn't be serious. But something about the crushed blackberry caught his sense of the ridiculous more than any other detail, and he started to giggle, at first in silence; the only sign was his body shaking. Mrs Lockwood noticed, frowned, dug him in the ribs, but with each succeeding absurdity from Mrs Wimbleball, the need to laugh out loud grew and grew.

"Colin!" his mother hissed. "Behave yourself!"

"I am!" he said, choking, and he almost fell off his seat. His foot knocked against the chair in front, and two ladies turned and said "Ssh!"

"Get out!" Mrs Lockwood muttered. "Get outside this instant! How dare you do this to me!"

Clutching his stomach and his mouth he ran from the room, through the area where the sherry party had been held, and dashed out into the street. He ran down St Martin's Lane, past the Ship Inn, and into Cathedral Yard, sped across the grass and only stopped by the west front of the cathedral itself, where he leaned against a buttress, and let out a great shout of laughter.

Moments later, when he had calmed down, he observed,

35

almost with surprise, that the sun had set; it would soon be dark. He remembered the jacket he had left on the top of the south tower; he might as well go in and fetch it, he thought, before the light failed completely.

Inside, the cathedral was a vast cavern of shadows in the dusk. There was no-one about, though the firewatchers must surely be somewhere in the building. The silence was enormous, sinister. A bat, flapping distractedly, almost made him whimper with fear.

He made his way up the spiral staircase more by touch on the stone than by seeing his way, then trod carefully along the catwalk above the roof of the nave. From the bellringers' room came the sound of voices; the door to it was edged by a thin oblong of light.

The students started in guilty surprise when he opened the door. There were eight of them, all playing poker. Colin explained his errand, and they told him they hadn't found his jacket, for none of them had yet been up on the battlements that evening. He noticed that they did their firewatching duties in comfort; on a table were piles of sandwiches, packets of cigarettes, and more than a dozen bottles of beer. Go on up, one of them said; he could look for it himself.

He was walking across the bell-chamber when he heard the air-raid warning. He had just reached the bell called Purdue. Lost. Nonsense, he said to himself, and put his hand, almost affectionately, on its cold metal. Should he forget his jacket, and hurry down, run out of the building while it was still safe? No. There was plenty of time, he knew that; there were always several minutes between the wailing of the sirens and the drone of approaching planes. The Nazi squadron – if indeed it was a squadron; it might only be a solitary fighter that had lost its way – would not have reached the coast yet; they would still be looking for Exmouth and the slit of the estuary to guide them.

He went on up.

The Lockwoods had not yet acquired a Morrison shelter, so on nights when there was an air-raid they slept in the cupboard under the stairs. It was cramped and uncomfortable, but they could, all five of them, just about squeeze in, as Mr Lockwood had pulled down the partition between the cupboard and the larder at the beginning of the war, thus trebling the amount of space. In fact they had never all found themselves in there at one and the same time, as the previous raids had occurred when Mary was on duty at the hospital. Mrs Lockwood had found the loss of her larder exceedingly inconvenient and grumbled a good deal about it at first: all her food had to be stored in a number of different places round the house, and the cupboard itself was hardly an ideal place to squat for an hour; she kept banging her head on the underneath of the stairs, or found the gas meter sticking into her hips. But after the first really severe raid she had not complained; it had occurred to her at last that this makeshift shelter might well save their lives.

Mr Lockwood was drinking tea when the sirens started their familiar unpleasant rise and fall. June was in the lavatory. Almost immediately they could hear the planes; for the first time the usual gap of ten or fifteen minutes between the warning and the arrival of the enemy had not occurred. The time of day was remarkable, too: nine o'clock in the evening, whereas all the previous raids had occurred in the small hours of the morning.

Damn, Mr Lockwood thought; it had to happen when his wife and two of his children were out in the city. Would they be all right? He supposed so; there was a shelter in the basement of Nimrod's, and there were at least two public shelters only a minute's walk from the Savoy Cinema. But it was worrying all the same. Would Lars and Mary, immersed in Deanna Durbin, even hear the siren? The cinema management might, but would they evacuate the audience immediately? Presumably. It wasn't certain, though; the problem, owing to the timing of the raid, had not previously occurred in Exeter.

"June! Come downstairs at once!" he shouted. The planes were now very near, Junkers he guessed from the noise, a jarring distortion like cars with holed exhaust boxes, amplified immensely. A very large force of them, many more than in previous raids. "June!!" She raced down the stairs, two at a time, and shot into the cupboard. The vibrations from the planes were causing the clock on the mantelpiece to ring out a thin high note in reply; B flat, Mr Lockwood, who had perfect pitch and a good singing voice, said to himself.

"Dad! Get in! What's the use of me being in here if you're standing outside? Come on!"

He looked round wildly, thinking he ought to throw some of the family's more valuable possessions into the shelter, but he could not decide what. He grabbed Brenda's fur coat from the hall-stand and two Enid Blyton books which were lying on the bottom step of the stairs. Then he rushed into the kitchen, picked up the half-drunk cups of tea, and dived into the cupboard, just as the shrill, ear-piercing whine of the first bomb to fall came from directly overhead.

The explosion seemed to pick the house up by its very foundations, hold it in the air for a fraction of a second, then drop it neatly back into place. June squealed, and threw herself into her father's arms. There was a great crashing of glass from upstairs, then rattling noises from the roof, followed by a sound that reminded Mr Lockwood of the sea; it was like shingle being dragged down the beach by a retreating wave.

"What is it?" June whispered.

"That noise? Plaster falling maybe. Cement, bits of stone."

"And the glass?"

"Our bedrooms, I think. And there were tiles smashing on the roof."

"Dad . . . I'm frightened."

He stroked her hair. "It wasn't us, was it? Somewhere in this road, I expect. But we're all right. Safe as houses." He smiled at the joke.

"What about Mum, and Colin, and – "

"I don't know." He untied his daughter's arms from around his neck. "Look. Let's keep calm. We'll drink our tea before it gets quite cold, shall we?"

The planes screamed overhead; one sounded as if it was plunging straight for the house, and just, it seemed, at the last possible moment, it swerved away, its roar dying in the distance. Every few moments there were explosions. Some were dull and flat, a thud, like a book dropping on the floor, or a distant door being slammed; some, weighing Heaven knew how many tons, reverberated right through the house even though they had obviously fallen a long way off, making ornaments jump and windows shake in their frames; some, not so heavy but nearer, produced a quite perceptible pause after the initial impact, then came the din of thousands of tons of bricks and stones collapsing (like thunder in a metal dustbin, June thought), wood ripping apart, and finally the lighter patter of dust and small stones showering on to the rubble.

"We've never had anything like this," said Mr Lockwood, almost to himself.

"Dad, that first one, the nearest. Do you think it was in our road?"

"It might have been."

39

"Who?"

"I don't know."

"The Mackenzies? The Bennetts? Could it be . . . the Hackmans? Or Mrs Penney?"

"June, I don't know! Don't think about it!"

"Dad . . . was it Pam?"

He pulled her towards him, and put his arm round her. "You mustn't say that," he said, softly. "She's probably in the shelter with her family, wondering if it was you. And she'd be wrong, love, wouldn't she? Just as you are, I'm certain." There was another explosion, very heavy, but distant, and the larder light immediately went out. He laughed. "At least we know where that one fell!"

"The power station?"

"Yes." He fumbled for the torch. It was kept on a hook, just inside the cupboard door.

"What's that red glow?"

"Where? Yes, you're right. It's fire!" She moved slightly, wanting to go out and look. "June, stay where you are!"

"Is it the city burning?"

"Not the city. Just a house, maybe two houses." And, as if to confirm it, there came from outside the strident clanging of a fire-engine bell. Another bomb dropped, just like the first, very near: the house shuddered but stayed intact, though there were noises from its various rooms, cups breaking in the kitchen, a chair overturning, something heavy in one of the bedrooms falling.

"Dad . . . why us? Why Exeter? Is it a Beandecker raid?"

"Baedecker, my love. It could be. Norwich, York, Bath. They've all been bombed recently, and there's nothing there except the cathedrals."

"The cathedrals!"

"Yes. That's what they're after, I'm afraid. I ought to be there, I – "

"Thank God you're not, Dad."

"Finish your tea."

The high-pitched metallic scream of a bomb: Mr Lockwood thought, this is it this time, this is it, it must be. He threw June roughly on to the floor, knocking over the tea-cups as he did so, and fell on top of her; there was a great cracking tearing noise as the roof split open, then they were both lifted up by the blast and hurled against the wall, every bone in their bodies shaken and battered, the uproar completely deafening them. The house disintegrated, an avalanche of bricks, wood, glass and dust.

The entrance to the underground passages, which were built in medieval times as a water conduit for the city, was only a minute's walk away from the cinema. Mary and Lars had wisely decided to take shelter there as soon as they heard the siren, though many of the audience watching the film stayed, believing perhaps the raid would be insignificant, a small affair on some distant part of the city or another probably unsuccessful attempt to sever the railway line at St David's. Or maybe they felt it was impossible that Hitler would strike while Deanna Durbin was singing. Large numbers of people, however, hurried to the underground passages from the Greyhound Inn and the flats over the High Street shops, and a queue formed at the entrance. There was no panic, even though the planes were now clearly visible and the first bombs were falling. But when St Lawrence's church, only a few hundred yards away, received a direct hit, and people were thrown backwards by the blast, there was a mad scramble down the steps. Lars and Mary were almost crushed and suffocated as the crowd tried to push its way to safety. A plane, very low, seemed to dive down towards them, like a huge bat silhouetted against the sky, and as it shot past there was a hail of bullets; chips of stone flew from the fronts of the nearest shops in puffs of dust, leaving white scars on the grimy walls.

"That was the gunner of the plane!" a man shouted. "They saw us; they're deliberately trying to mow us down!"

At last they were inside. It was cold, clammy, and pitch dark in the narrow passageways and the walls were wet. They could hear the occasional drip of water despite the barrage of aeroplane noise and buildings collapsing. Someone produced a torch, and in its faint glimmer, Mary could see people ahead of her as far as the light would reach, standing as if in a queue for an unexpected delivery of tomatoes or some similar, usually unobtainable, delicacy at the greengrocer's. Men, women, and children stood, patiently now that the stampede was over, in complete silence, too dazed to utter a word. Were Dad and June safe, Mary wondered, in the cupboard under the stairs? Suppose the house was crushed under a direct hit! No, she must not think that, she must not start to panic: the odds against it were surely enormous, weren't they? And Colin and Mum at Nimrod's? Well, there was a proper shelter there, of course. No, it was Dad and June she feared for most. Try as she might, she could not push out of her head a picture of her little sister, pinned under a fallen beam or a heap of smashed bricks, bleeding, screaming for help.

Lars, from behind, put his arms round her. His mouth was against her ear. She turned, slowly and carefully, in order not to disturb the person in front – it was the woman holding the torch – and then Lars was kissing her, not as he sometimes kissed her goodnight or a gentle brush of the lips in the privacy of the cinema, but properly.

The torch flashed on their faces. "Here, Ethel! Look at these two!" The voice was that of a Londoner. "Some folk get at it anywhere it's dark!" There was laughter from the people nearby, and Mary, acutely embarrassed, extricated herself from Lars's arms.

"I'm sorry," she said, rather primly.

"Here, duck, no need to apologise! Make the most of it, I say, handsome bloke like that! If you don't, there's others that will! Ain't that right, Ethel?" There were more laughs, and Mary felt herself blushing a deep crimson. Then, suddenly, a murmur of conversation came from all parts of the crowd: the initial shock produced by the raid had been dispelled. The torch-owner, Mary noticed, was middle-aged and extremely fat. "We was in a shelter every night of the London blitz," she said, "and there was some rum goings-on then I can tell you. So don't you worry yourself, love. Yes. Evacuated down here for a bit of peace and quiet and country air. Heavitree. Never heard of it, so I said to meself Hitler won't have, neither. Blimey, we was wrong, wasn't we! Gawd, what was that?" There was an explosion very close to, and the blast waves burst into the passages, cannoning people forwards into each other.

"Are we safe in here?" Mary asked, anxiously.

"I don't know," Lars answered. He put his arms round her again.

"I hope it wasn't the Savoy," said Ethel, the torch-owner's friend. She was just as fat, and was eating her way through a bag of peanuts. "If it was we'll never see that Deanna Durbin. Bought these in the interval," she explained.

Did he love her? It wasn't possible to say such a thing in circumstances like these, underground in a wet tunnel packed with people. No. It was possible. You could say something like that anywhere, surely; time and place were of no importance at all. She thought of her women's magazine stories and tried to find

43

some reassuring parallel, but all those heroes and heroines declared their feelings on yachts under star-studded skies in the Mediterranean, or at dinner in expensive restaurants half-way up mountains at ski-resorts. Sometimes, of course, there were romantic characters like ballet-dancers, and the heroines were often nurses, girls without money or background, but whose virtues shone so dazzlingly that the young heir to the chateau was blinded with passion.

He didn't love her. That was obvious. Just a girl to go around with in that twilight part of his life, the few weeks before call-up.

Perhaps she didn't love him. Perhaps she had been hoodwinked by all those visions of ballerinas in tu-tus: stage moonlight, Les Sylphides, arabesques, czardases. No. She did love him. Even though it was hopeless. Quite hopeless.

"I ought to be at the hospital," she said, as another explosion rocked the tunnel. "There will be hundreds of casualties. Lord, why didn't I think of it before?" Into her mind's eye flashed a picture of her father and June, lifeless or dying, on stretchers under grey blankets, being carried from the ruins of the house. "Lars . . . Dad, June . . . do you think they're all right?"

"I don't know."

"But suppose the house has been bombed! There's no real shelter. They might be dead!"

"Mary, calm down!"

"I must get to the hospital! I should have thought of it before!"

"I did."

"Why ever didn't you say?"

"And have you killed on the way there? Just listen to it!" The din outside was terrifying: planes seeming to tear the sky to pieces as they swooped, turned, and flew in again to attack; the

44

bombs detonating; the thunder of falling masonry. The only sounds from above which suggested that life in the city continued were occasional blasts of an air-raid warden's whistle, running feet, the distant bell of a fire-engine or an ambulance.

"Lars, I ought to go!"

He put his arms against the walls, blocking her way. "I'm not going to let you out. You'll have to struggle. That will be nice!"

"Lars!"

"Go on, then. What's one nurse less? I shouldn't think it will have much effect on the war effort. Of course you might not be killed. You could be so badly injured that a whole team of doctors and nurses would be needed to save your life. I suppose it might divert them from other things, like treating the injured and dying." He took his arms away from the walls, and said "Go on. I'm not stopping you."

"All right," she said, wearily. "I'll stay."

"Well, duck? Having a good time?" It was the woman with the torch. She had just finished reminiscing with her friend about the most fearsome night of the London blitz. They agreed that it wasn't much worse than the present air-raid. "Don't you worry, love. When the all-clear goes and we get out of here you'll find it ain't so bad as you think. Always sounds worse than it is. They ain't so clever, them Nazi bombers. You wait and see."

Four

THE AIR-RAID WARNING sounded quite clearly in the inner sanctum of Nimrod's, but Mrs Wimbleball only looked up briefly to say "Oh, take no notice, my dears. I was doing a show in Coventry when the bombs were showering down all over the place! We just carried on! Now, for next to *no* coupons this multi-striped reverse-knit sweater with vertical rib . . . Oh . . .!" The noise of Junker fighter-bombers growing louder and louder seemed unaccountably to distract the minds of the audience away from next autumn's clothes: there was an anxious buzz of conversation; people began to stand up and move towards the door.

"The shelter's in the basement!" Miss Garland shouted. "Stairs on the left of the front entrance, or there's a lift just behind the curtain over there! Mrs Wimbleball, I think we should . . . er . . ."

"Of *course*, my dear, I understand. Daphne darling, if you'd just switch off the projector. Don't rewind the film; we can resume when . . ." But Daphne, more concerned for her own safety, was already disappearing out of the room.

Mrs Lockwood followed the majority of the customers who were making for the stairs. She was alarmed not to see Colin in the outer room of the shop; she had expected to find him there,

46

still collecting up glasses and empty plates. The first bombs fell, some distance away, but the noise and the tremors that shook the floor and walls were sufficient to cause a rush for the staircase.

"There's nothing to worry about!" shouted Mr Kitchen. "In orderly fashion, please, everybody! We'll be quite safe if we all keep calm!" He seemed to think he should be in control, being one of the few males among a crowd of women who were almost certain to run amok at any moment. He placed himself at the top of the staircase, and tried to stop people jostling and shoving, for all the world as if he was at school on playground duty.

Mrs Lockwood hurried back through the shop and into the toilet where there was a hand-basin; perhaps Colin was in there, washing up the glasses. He wasn't. She returned to the outer room, and ran into the street, just as St Lawrence's church, a few hundred yards further down, crumbled, with a brilliant flash of light and a tremendous roar, into a heap of rubble. The blast wave, at this distance, was not too fierce, but she remembered, before it hit her, to open her mouth in case it damaged her eardrums. She was blown backwards a little, rather as if she had turned a corner in a high wind and unexpectedly walked into the full force of a gale. All the glass in Nimrod's shop-front seemed to curve inwards, so that instead of being vertical, the windows, for a fraction of a second, appeared to be semicircular: then they snapped back into place. Not one pane was cracked. An optical illusion, she reassured herself, as she anxiously looked about for Colin. No sign. Where on earth could he be? Even if he had left the shop immediately after she had turned him out of the show he would not have had time to reach home; in fact he might not have decided to go home. She hadn't told him to do so. Where was he? He could be anywhere in the

47

city, anywhere! She could never credit him with much sense, but surely he would have run to the nearest shelter? Wouldn't he? Suppose he didn't know where it was? Suppose he panicked? No, Colin wouldn't panic. He wasn't the type. Would June and Ron be safe under the stairs? And Lars and Mary in the cinema? They'd never hear the siren in there! Whatever should she do for the best?

A plane screamed low overhead and machine-gun bullets spurted little holes in a line along the pavement. She fled into the shop. It was empty now, the neat rows of chairs she had laid out that afternoon scattered in all directions.

"Brenda! Come here this *instant*!" It was Mrs Wimbleball, in the lift; behind her were another woman and the man who had been ordering people about at the top of the stairs. "I'm going to shut these doors! Come on before it's too late!"

"I'm looking for Colin! My son!"

"That nice young man who served the sherry?"

"Have you seen him?"

"No. But I'm sure he's all right. Come on, Brenda! *Hurry*!"

Mrs Lockwood hesitated, but the whine of a bomb falling, uncomfortably close, decided her, and she dashed into the lift.

"Going down," said Mrs Wimbleball, and she slammed the gate shut. There was a colossal explosion nearby, hurling the four of them against each other; Mrs Lockwood's head hit Mrs Wimbleball's so violently that stars danced in front of her eyes. The light flickered, went out, and the lift stopped moving. "Drat!" said Mrs Wimbleball. "We're stuck between floors."

"We must call for help!" cried Mrs Lockwood, and she pressed all the buttons, but nothing happened.

"There's no point," said the man. "Everyone will be in your shelter; they'll hardly venture out with this kind of raid going on. Allow me to introduce myself. Percy Kitchen, and this is my wife, Rosemary."

"Oh, you teach my son, Colin Lockwood."

"Yes. I do have that . . . er . . . pleasure."

"Mr Kitchen, I hope you won't mind me saying so, but . . . er . . . that essay you set him, the punishment —"

"I'd hardly expect him to do it now. Not after this. As a matter of fact, strictly between you and me, I shouldn't have given it to him in the first place. Rosemary and I have had a very trying day. Our house was badly damaged last night, not a direct hit, but we've had to move out; it's structurally unsafe. Lost an awful lot of stuff. An awful lot. And hardly a wink of sleep . . . a full timetable to teach. Colin was just the last straw, I'm afraid. He's not very good at history, not exactly an academic . . . but that doesn't mean I ought to take it out on him . . . I just saw red, I suppose. Silly of me."

"We came here tonight to cheer ourselves up," said Mrs Kitchen. "I've lost nearly all my clothes. We can't usually afford Nimrod fashions; I just thought it would take my mind off things, seeing some really nice coats and dresses."

"Why are we all standing?" Mrs Wimbleball asked. "It looks as if we're going to be here for *centuries*, so we might as well make ourselves comfortable." It was very cramped, but they all managed eventually to sit. "Mrs Kitchen, do you mind if I move my knees? Ah, that's better!" She fumbled in her handbag. "I always carry a bottle of brandy with me in case of emergencies. This is undoubtedly an emergency." She unscrewed the cap. "Black market, of course." She took a large swig and coughed. "Lovely! You can feel it tingling, Brenda, right down inside." She offered it to the others, who refused. "Ah well, all the more for me," she said, and put it back in her handbag.

"I'm scared out of my wits about Colin," said Mrs Lockwood. "If he has—"

"Brenda darling, you mustn't flap! He's bound to be safe. You must have *masses* of shelters in Exeter!"

"We haven't. That's the trouble." Mrs Lockwood, despite her anxieties, wanted to giggle; it was easy to understand why Colin had gone into convulsions.

"The city centre's taking a beating," Mr Kitchen said, as an explosion swung the lift from side to side, banging it against the walls of the shaft. "Are we far from the bottom? I was wondering what would happen if the cable snapped."

"It can't be more than a few feet," Mrs Lockwood said. "It's the least of our worries." She suddenly realised that, in her fears for Colin, she had almost forgotten that the other members of her family might be in danger equally great, that the house might have been hit, that June or Ron might be dead or badly injured, and there was nothing, absolutely nothing, that she could do about it. The full horror of the situation struck her so forcibly that she almost screamed.

"Brenda! I've asked you twice! Are you sure it's only a few feet?"

"Yes . . . yes . . ."

"Thank God for that!" Mrs Wimbleball heaved a sigh of relief. "I had visions of being *whirled* hundreds of feet to an absolutely certain death!" She wriggled and fidgeted. "So sorry, Brenda, but my arm's gone to sleep." There was a long silence; everyone was lost in their own worries. "This is too morbid for words," Mrs Wimbleball said eventually. "Let's drown that wretched racket. I think we should all sing something."

"Good idea," said Mr Kitchen.

So the four of them sang "Run, rabbit, run", "There'll always be an England", and "The white cliffs of Dover". They had just started on "We're gonna hang out the washing on the Siegfried Line" when there was an ear-splitting crash from above; a huge beam of wood smashed through the roof of the lift, and they were buried under hundreds of tons of falling masonry.

Colin found his jacket still there, quite safe. He was about to return down the spiral staircase when he heard the sound of planes. He leaned on the battlements and looked towards the south, down the river; there they were, tiny gnats on the horizon, but growing larger every second. German aircraft! He had never seen a formation of them, not in real life, only at the flicks. Black crosses against the sky: he began counting them, but there were too many. Wave after wave of them, strikingly clear, for it was not yet dark, and the moon was already brilliant. It did not occur to him that he should be terrified, even when the first J.U. 88s flew low overhead: he was mesmerised by the sight; it was awesome, almost beautiful. He could see the hatches open, and the bombs tumbling out; the first fell harmlessly in the river, then one exploded in a street in St Thomas; another demolished a shop by the Lower Market. The cathedral shuddered. A column of black smoke rose over Mary Arches Street, and the planes veered away. Then the second wave was upon the city. Hundreds of tiny objects falling: incendiary bombs. Four landed on the roof of the quire below him, and at once the fire-watchers were on the scene, hurrying from doors in the two towers that he had not previously noticed.

Why was he not afraid, he asked himself? Was he so numb with shock that he could not move, could not feel? Was this being "rooted to the spot", a phrase he'd often read when someone was transfixed with horror by an assassination or an act of dreadful brutality? Was it? No. He didn't feel anything, except

51

this overwhelming desire to see, to experience. He watched a plane screech down low, over London Inn Square, heard the crack of machine-gun bullets on stone. St Lawrence's church blew apart, then an oil bomb, he thought, to judge by the flames, hit St Luke's College. Now there were explosions all round, too many to count, too many to note precisely what had been struck. And there were fires everywhere.

Mum safe in the basement of Nimrod's. June and Dad safe in the cupboard under the stairs, provided the house held up, of course. He looked in that direction, but it was impossible to see whether bombs had fallen there or not; there was too much smoke. They should have had a proper shelter; why hadn't somebody done something about it before now! He thought of his father, dying in the blazing rubble, then shook his head in disbelief. No. He concentrated on Mary and Lars. No, Dad and June would be all right. Wouldn't they? They had to be . . . Dad! Mary and Lars, yes, they would surely have run over to the underground passages. The passages! The gunner of a plane was aiming his bullets at the entrance! Mum would be demented wondering where he was. He ought to sprint back down the tower, and . . . across Cathedral Yard, up St Martin's Lane, up the High Street to Nimrod's? Just to assure her he was all right? That would be madness. Any number of buildings could fall on him; a plane gunner might spot him and shoot him dead as he ran; flying debris and shrapnel could mutilate him.

It was also madness, he knew, to stay where he was, but he felt extraordinarily safe on the roof of the tower. There was no fear of anything collapsing on him; just to think of it falling, himself underneath it, those bells crashing downwards, was more than enough to make him tremble. He would be pulverised beyond all recognition. Yet it was quite absurd to stay, because if the tower disintegrated, he would be killed just the same, instantly, shattered to pieces.

Exeter was burning. The whole top end of the High Street was on fire, a mass of flame and smoke. Bedford Circus was ablaze, so was Sidwell Street, South Street, the Lower Market. He could see whole shop fronts, several storeys high, crack, tilt, totter, then subside to the ground like a heap of toy bricks.

The planes flew in again, from all sides it seemed. A bullet nicked the corner of one of the battlements, missing him by inches. He shrank back into the doorway at the top of the staircase, and saw, out of the corner of his eye, a dark shape drop down, away to his right. He was thinking that the blast-waves up here were much fainter than if he had been down on the ground, only puffs of an unnaturally warm breeze blowing from one direction after another, when an enormous explosion almost deafened him and a great invisible force picked him up and flung him on to the pyramid of lead in the centre of the tower. I'm still here, he thought; I'm not hurt, though there was pain in his knees and his groin. I didn't hit my face on the lead. Keep your mouth open, another blast-wave! It struck him, totally flattening him, like the cat colliding with the wall in those silly cartoon films, and he had a sudden vision of himself as two-dimensional, a thing of cardboard, and a moment's sense of weightlessness, as he imagined it would feel in space or on the moon.

He was on his feet, astonished at how unnerved he felt with the shock. His best suit was filthy, ripped at both knees. He staggered towards the battlements, clutching on to the stone to support himself, and peered over. A direct hit on the cathedral: it had demolished the chapel of St James, and two of the buttresses. All the glass in the great quire windows had been blown out, but, amazingly, all the tracery, as far as he could see, was intact. The debris was still settling, stone falling from unstable

53

snapped-off ribs of the vault. Unstable! The quire itself stood, its massive pillars apparently unshaken. Suppose those pillars were now dangerously weakened? Then the whole of the quire might crash into rubble and dust, half of Exeter's great glory in ruins. That decided him. He had better get out while he could, risk the possibility of the building falling on him during the minutes the journey would take him; get out of here, run, find shelter. He wondered why it was he could see everything in such detail, the fluting on the pillars, the gargoyles on the parapets. Then he realised: the fire. The city was brilliantly illuminated, almost as clearly as in daylight.

There was a body on the roof below, one of the student fire-watchers, sprawled, on his back.

Colin ran down the stairs into the bell-chamber and stopped, surprised by the noise. The vibrations had caused the bells to hum, a toneless continuous buzzing like an angry swarm of bees. He put his hand on the cold metal of Doom, then Purdue. Not yet. Not yet. Then on, down through the bell-ringers' room, along the cat-walk, and, at last, the spiral staircase to the nave. There people were running in all directions, shouting orders, carrying buckets, fixing a hose. No-one paid him any attention. The air was filled with acrid choking stone-dust. The vault flickered in the fire-light: the fan-shaped spines of stone seemed to be alive, to be waving gently, like palm trees breathing in a vast conservatory. Everywhere on the floor lay broken glass, fragments from wall-tablets, bits of the columns of the bombed chapel, scattered by the blast. He passed by the memorial his ancestor had carved. It was covered in cracks, and several pieces, including the name at the bottom right-hand corner, were missing.

He glanced at the floor and saw it at once, a thin triangle. There was no-one looking his way. He picked it up and slipped

it into his pocket, then raced out of the building. He had a frag-
ment of history, all his own. That would confound Kitchen, the
old fossil! Not even he, in his long and rotten life, would ever
have come into possession – illegally or otherwise – of a stone
with his great-great-something-grandfather's name on it! He
took it out of his pocket and stared at it. The letters danced in
the light of the flames. Paul Sanders, mason.

About an hour and a half after the first bomb fell the all-clear
sounded. The people in the underground passages, very cold
and stiff from the cramped positions in which they had been
standing – the floor had been too wet and slimy to sit on –
began to shuffle slowly up the steps and out into the open air.
They needed no torches to find their way, for at first glance the
city appeared to be on fire from end to end. And totally trans-
formed. The entrance to the passages was in a maze of narrow
lanes and alleyways, a stone's throw from the High Street shops;
it was an area of tall old buildings, mostly Victorian, but some
older. Nothing remained except wrecked walls and heaps of
burning rubble. The Savoy Cinema no longer existed. Dimly,
through the smoke, the towers of the cathedral could be seen,
black silhouettes against a background of fire.

It was difficult to breathe. People choked and spluttered as
they looked for a path through the ruins, or tried to recognise
familiar objects in this desolate new landscape. It seemed almost
impossible to find a way that would avoid the flames. There was
no sign of any fire-engines. When someone asked, bitterly,
whether all the firemen were asleep or drinking tea, an air-raid
warden, who was hurrying by, stopped and said that so many
streets were blocked by piles of debris that it was quite impossible for the fire-engines to get through. For the moment,
the city would have to be left to burn. "You must all get out of

here," he shouted to the crowd, and a blazing length of timber crashed to the ground to reinforce his point.

"Where? How? Which way?" people asked.

He waved his arm towards a huge mass of stone and wood which was not alight. "Pick your way through that and you'll find Southernhay relatively clear."

Several men came into view, clambering down the ruins the warden had indicated. They were carrying crowbars, pick-axes and spades. "We need more volunteers!" one of them shouted.

"Women and children please go!" the warden yelled. "As many men as possible are needed here. There are several people buried under this," and he pointed at the blazing wreckage of the Greyhound Inn.

"I'll stay," Lars said.

"Come to the hospital as soon as you can," said Mary. "Please go and find out if the rest of the family are safe, Lars. And come and tell me."

"We must shift that too." The warden looked at the rubble which was obstructing the top end of Southernhay. Many of the people who had been sheltering in the passages were now climbing over it. "If we can dig a path through there the firemen may be able to get in. Problem is Fore Street and Sidwell Street are impassable, so are Magdalen Street and the Topsham Road."

"What about the hospital?" Mary asked.

"City Hospital's been gutted by incendiaries. R.D. and E.'s not touched, as far as I know."

She made her way over the debris. It was not easy; what looked like a firm foothold turned out to be a tiny brick hiding a gaping hole, or a massive piece of stone she thought she could cling to teetered and wobbled dangerously. Just like her own house might be, she thought. For the hundredth time she thought of June and Dad buried under a mound of rubble just like this one, and she had to suppress her overwhelming desire to run home and find out. Her first duty was to the hospital, she told herself. Lars would come with the news soon enough. She eventually arrived on the other side, her only mishaps being a broken finger-nail and a tear in her dress. Her hands and clothes were filthy with dust and soot. Southernhay, a long wide street of elegant eighteenth-century terraces, with a stretch of grass, trees and flower-beds along the length of its centre, had not escaped damage. A whole row of fine old houses had been smashed to pieces; there were little fires burning in the rubble. A tree was alight. She was able to run now, hindered only by broken glass and fallen roof-tiles. The Royal Devon and Exeter Hospital, at the far end of the street, was virtually unharmed, apart from a number of broken windows. She paused on the steps to get her breath, and looked across to the cathedral. There were two great fires, not one. Bedford Circus and the whole top end of the High Street and its surrounding area were engulfed in flames, and a smaller though equally frightening blaze was destroying Fore Street and South Street. In between stood the cathedral, the houses and shops of Cathedral Yard, and the church of St Mary Major; they formed an island that had, apparently, survived.

She cleaned herself up and reported for duty. It proved to be the longest night she had ever known. She worked non-stop till dawn, worrying all the while about her family and hoping they weren't terrified out of their minds about her. It was unthinkable, however, to take time off, go out and inquire; there was far too much to do in the hospital. If only Lars would come and let her know! Where was he? Casualty after casualty was brought in. Some of the injuries were terrible: faces that would be disfigured for ever by flying glass, lacerated arms, crushed legs, children blinded, bodies burned beyond recognition but still just gasping for life. There were makeshift beds in every corridor, even on the corners of staircases. While patients who needed immediate surgery were attended to, others had to wait, groaning with suffering.

A young man was brought in on a stretcher; he was wearing a greatcoat, and appeared to be in little pain. He was treated for shock as there was no apparent injury, no sign of blood on his clothes. He was placed on a chair out of the way; Mary gave him little thought other than wondering why he seemed so remarkably pale. She forgot him as she went about her duties, but an hour later she passed by, and noticed that he was slumped over the arm of the chair. She lifted him up, but he fell back; she felt his pulse: nothing. She unbuttoned the greatcoat, then, used though she was by now to the sight of hideous mutilations, screamed with horror. His body was almost totally severed at the top of both legs. A doctor, hurrying by, took charge, and Mary was called away to see to other patients, so she never discovered what exactly had happened, or why no-one, herself included, despite the haste and desperation in which the hospital staff were working, had seen at once what was wrong with him.

But a worse shock was to follow. A woman was carried in; she was laughing and joking with the stretcher-bearers despite the pain that was clearly registered on her ashen face. Though she had never met her, Mary knew at once from the accent and the language that this was Mrs Wimbleball. Behind her, on another stretcher, was Mrs Lockwood, unconscious and bleeding profusely.

"What's happened? Mum!! What . . ." But the men, grim and unsmiling, did not stop to answer her questions.

Mrs Wimbleball turned her head slightly. "Nothing to fret over," she said. "Brenda will be all right. You must be little

Miriam. Oh, what a *bore*! I think I'm going to be sick." But she was not; she fainted instead.

Mary soon heard the full story, from one of the stretcher-bearers, who paused on his way out to grab a quick cup of tea. Only the front wall and some steel girdering were left of Nimrod's, and this was so unsafe that it would have to be pulled down as soon as possible. All the customers who had attended the fashion-show and who had taken shelter in the basement were unhurt, though they had had to be dug out from under the remains of the shop. The casualties were four people found in the wreckage of the lift, which had been crushed to a third of its original size. Two of them, a man and his wife, identified as a Mr and Mrs Kitchen, had been killed. The others had been extraordinarily lucky; a huge beam of wood had smashed the lift, but had lodged flat only inches away from them and it had supported the masonry that had fallen on top. One of them, the talkative lady, had multiple fractures in both legs. The other woman was suffering, he thought, from some internal injury; he couldn't say what. The talkative lady was quite a character; all she seemed to be worried about was her film, and that was the amazing thing, it was still in its projector, not a mark on it, just a little dust . . .

But Mary didn't wait to hear the rest; she ran off to find out news of her mother. Mrs Lockwood, she was told, was not badly hurt. She had lost a lot of blood from a long deep incision in her left side, caused by a piece of flying metal; there was also bruising, minor cuts: but no reason to suppose she would not fully recover.

During the course of the night grim pieces of news filtered through to those on duty at the hospital. Bedford Circus, Exeter's most beautiful street, was almost totally destroyed. The fires in the High Street and South Street were uncontrollable. It

59

was said the flames could be seen from thirty miles away. The cathedral was damaged, though not severely. Outside the city centre there was a great deal of devastation too; St Luke's College gutted by fire bombs, whole areas of Newtown and St Sidwell's, little streets of shoddy Victorian houses, flattened. There was no light, water or gas. At least the hospital had its own electricity generator, though water was a dreadful problem.

Lars arrived as dawn was breaking. His clothes were torn and filthy; his face unshaven and covered in grime, his eyes bloodshot. Mary, almost asleep on her feet, put her head on his shoulder and sobbed her heart out. "Mum's in here, injured. But where's Colin? He's missing!"

Five

IT WAS JUNE who recovered her wits first. When the last deafening noises of the house collapsing had subsided, she told herself
to stop being frightened; they were alive: then she thought, all
the house couldn't have fallen; it just somehow didn't feel as if it
had. She listened for a moment as small objects trickled and
bumped through the holes between the bricks and wood above,
then she wriggled herself free from her father, groped for the
torch, found it, and switched it on. Dad was sitting cross-legged
against the wall in a cloud of whirling grey dust, clutching his
head, a dazed expression on his face.

"Are you all right, Dad?" She pulled at the cupboard door,
but it would not open. "What's the matter with it? Ugh, the
dust! I can hardly breathe!"

"We're not dead. I don't understand." There were more
bombs, dull thuds across the other side of the city.

"Of course we're not dead. Not hurt, either. Well, a bit
bruised."

"I've got a headache. I hit something. But I can't feel anything wrong with me." He coughed and choked.

"Help me with this door."

"I shouldn't touch it. Wait till people come and dig us out."

But at that moment the door burst open as she tugged it, and a torrent of rubbish poured in, mostly broken bricks, cement and bits of the ceiling, but also some unlikely articles: two bent tea-spoons that should have been in the sideboard drawer and a brass candlestick from the dining-room mantelpiece. "Now," she said, "let's see if we can fight our way through."

"I don't think we should. In fact, I forbid it, June! You could disturb some fallen beam out there and a whole lot more rubble might come crashing down." He choked again, held his hand to his mouth. "You've made it much worse opening that door."

"I'll just have a little look." She lay on the debris that had cas-caded into the cupboard, and shone the torch out: splintered wood, twisted metal, triangles of jagged glass, and a large curved porcelain thing, cracked but otherwise unbroken. "The lavatory pan!" she exclaimed. "I can see the lavatory! It's about half-way between the hall floor and the ceiling; I mean where the ceiling used to be! Well, I never!"

"Well you never, do you! What else?"

"Torn material. My bedroom curtains I think they are. There's a light bulb. And some food. It could be butter, all squashed; I'm not sure." She waved the torch about. "Dad! I can see the sky! Surely . . . surely that's a star!"

"Let me look." He crawled over, and they changed places. "You're right, my girl! You're right! That must mean . . . the house can't be completely wrecked. If it was, we'd be buried so deep we couldn't see out at all! That explains it, perhaps."

"Explains what?"

"Why we weren't killed. Why the staircase stood up to it." He shone the torch in different directions, peered this way and that. "I think it's only the back that's gone," he said eventually. "Your bedroom and Colin's, the bathroom and lavatory, they've collapsed into the kitchen and the dining-room. But the rest of the house is still there." He sniffed. "Do you smell anything strange?"

"Yes. I think it's gas." Planes droned overhead: not the scream now of dive-bombers; it was a steady sound, fading away.

"Mmm. Mains leak. Could be very dangerous."

"Then we've *got* to climb out, Dad! Honestly I'd feel much safer if we tried, I would really. I . . ."

"What is it, love?"

"I'm frightened in here. In case something else falls down, I mean. Suppose another bomb hit the front of the house?"

"The odds against that must be pretty high. However, we don't want to be poisoned by coal gas." He started to move. "I'll go first, and –"

"I ought to go first. I'm smaller, and I'll dislodge less stuff. You might knock all sorts of things down on me."

Mr Lockwood thought about that, then reluctantly agreed. "Take the torch," he said. "And be very careful, June. Very careful."

She eased her way out slowly. It wasn't anything like as difficult as she had imagined; a bit like being in the middle of a hedge, she thought, except that instead of unstitching brambles from her clothes or trampling nettles underfoot or gingerly taking hawthorn twigs out of her hair, it was removing vicious glass splinters, or pushing pieces of twisted piping aside, or edging round the kitchen dresser without making it wobble.

"I'm out!" she cried triumphantly, as she stood on the top of the rubble. "The front of the house *is* still standing! And Dad! Exeter's on fire! There's a huge blaze right in the city centre!"

"What about the cathedral?"

"Still there. I can see the towers, at any rate."

"Thank God." He heaved a sigh of relief. "June! Stop spinning that blessed torch around! Do you want the Germans to find out where we are? Shine it down here so I can see what I'm doing." He slipped, and several bricks and pieces of broken white china fell, then something dropped very heavily and painfully on his feet. "Bloody. . . !" June grinned to herself as he uttered a whole string of words she had only ever heard from nasty rough boys in the school playground, words she was surprised her father even knew. "Sorry about that," he said at last. "The dining-room clock fell on my right foot." He kicked it away with his left foot, and, obligingly it started to chime, faltered after three bongs and proceeded to go through all the quarters, one after the other, backwards. Just as it had finished its strange recital, the confident rising wail of the all-clear sounded.

"We're safe! We're safe!" June shouted. "They've gone!"

"I'm not safe till I'm out of here." Mr Lockwood was trying to squeeze past the kitchen dresser, but he was larger than June, and he had to tilt it slightly. The movement upset its precarious balance, and it fell over with a tremendous noise as all its contents — jars, plates and glasses — smashed into each other. A whole lot more debris became unsettled and tumbled down on top of it. Fortunately this widened the tunnel through which he was crawling, instead of blocking it and burying him securely underneath as he had feared. His journey was now relatively easy. Soon he and June were standing on the firm ground of the back garden.

"Look at that," she said, shining the torch on to a wall of the house which was still standing, more or less intact. There was nothing left of the bathroom, not a trace of its floor or ceiling or windows, but stuck firmly to the wall, unscathed and secure, was the bath. "I've never seen its underneath before," she added. "It's got claws. I never realised."

"Oh dear, oh dear, oh dear!" he said. "But it does look so

funny! Just imagine yourself with nothing on, having a good scrub, when the bomb exploded. What a shock you'd have had! Like Marat's murder!"

The idea made June laugh as well, but they both stopped when a voice nearby called out "What's so amusing? Have you both gone crazy?" It was Pam's father, Mr Foster, and behind him a crowd of neighbours were gathered, all wondering what was going on. June explained, and everybody looked up and joined in the joke. "We'll ask the city council to preserve it as a monument," said Mr Foster. "A memorial befitting the great and mighty Adolf." Then he sobered up, and told Mr Lockwood that the bomb which had partially destroyed the house had scored a direct hit on old Miss Chadwick's next door. They were digging in the ruins now, but there was little chance, he thought, of finding her alive. His own house had stood up well, he said, just broken windows and slates off the roof. June and her father had better come and stay the night there. Pam would be delighted to see them; she was in a dreadful state, thinking that June might have been killed. But . . . where was the rest of the family?

Mr Lockwood said he hoped his wife and Colin were in Nimrod's shelter, and Mary, if she hadn't been hurt, would most likely have gone to the hospital. He was going to Nimrod's now, then the hospital, and if all was well he would try and reach the cathedral if it was possible. He didn't know what time he would be back, but June, yes, should certainly stay at Pam's if Mrs Foster didn't mind.

June went off with Mr Foster, and Mr Lockwood, anxious and depressed, set out for the city centre. The relief at finding himself and June unharmed had passed. His headache was worse, and the pain in his foot was so severe that he could only limp slowly. His fears for his family grew as he approached the

High Street. The fires were much bigger than he would have guessed from Denmark Road, and as he turned into Southernhay, a shower of sparks and a wave of intense heat were wafted towards him on the wind. Brenda, Mary, Colin, trapped in that inferno, burned to death perhaps! He forgot his own aches and pains and ran towards the heap of debris that blocked the entrance into the High Street.

A plane was diving straight at him. All around machine-gun bullets leapt from the tarmac, or embedded themselves in the grass outside the cathedral. Colin, galvanised into action, raced to the porch of St Mary Major. There was a slight pain in his left arm; a bullet had made two neat round holes, its points of entry and exit, in the sleeve of his jacket, and had left a long horizontal cut in his skin. It didn't hurt much, but the blood was trickling down his arm, staining his hand. The nearest public shelter was in South Street. He must get there as quickly as possible: it would be ridiculous to be killed now, after the adventures he had already experienced, quite absurd.

There was a lull; the planes had all swept over the city and were turning, somewhere to the north, in order to swoop down for another attack. The obvious way out here was impossible; the little path that led from St Mary Major was obstructed by debris from the College of Vicars Choral, which appeared to have received a direct hit. In any case, the street beyond was on fire; the heat was too intense to let him through.

He ran back towards the cathedral and into Palace Gate. There was no damage here, apart from the choir school which had been bombed last month; in two minutes he was out in South Street by the White Hart public house. This seemed to mark the edge of the destruction, and in less than no time he was scuttling down the steps of a shelter by Holy Trinity church.

"Look what the cat's brought in!" said a familiar voice. It was Terry Wootton. Colin was too breathless to answer, and Wootton, he could see, was curious to know what he was doing there: in a moment he would ask, "Done your history homework, then, Lockwood?"

Colin showed him the piece of stone with his ancestor's name carved on it. "My great-great-great-*great*-grandfather," he said, though he was not sure if he had put in too many 'greats'.

Wootton looked at it, then said, "Anyone can pick up an old bit of stone and say it's his great-great-great-great-grandfather's. I bet you can't prove it."

"I don't *have* to prove it. I *know*."

"Where did you find it, then?"

"Mind your own flipping business." The blood on his hand was now quite worthy of comment; he was aware Wootton had noticed and he knew that if he was patient, a question was sure to come.

"Dog bitten you?"

"Machine-gun bullet," Colin said, in as nonchalant a tone as he could muster.

Wootton laughed. "You don't reckon I'm going to swallow that, do you?"

Colin rolled up his sleeve and showed what sort of wound it was, a long clean line through the surface of the flesh, nothing like an animal bite. He pointed to the holes in the cloth. "That's where it went in," he said, "and that's where it went out. It's stuck in the east wall of St Mary Major if you want to go and look for it. You can always have it analysed by forensic experts if you're that interested."

Wootton was silent, trying unsuccessfully to hide the fact that he was deeply impressed. He had heard the sound of machine-gun fire and had guessed that the German planes were trying to shoot down anyone they could catch a glimpse of.

Colin looked round. The shelter was a sea of faces, most of them gazing at him curiously; there was no electricity, and light came from candles and an old-fashioned storm-lantern. It made the people seem like figures in some old painting of the birth of Christ.

"What's happening out there?" a young girl asked, and Colin suddenly felt it was strange that they hadn't questioned him before. They were a depressing crowd, silent, stupefied almost; still, if they had had to put up with Wootton for the whole of the air-raid, it wasn't surprising.

"Cathedral's had a direct hit. Not a bad one, I think. It's knocked a hole in the side of the quire, that's all. I don't know much else. The whole top end of this street's flattened and most of it's burning."

"That's what we thought," said the person on the other side of Wootton. She was grey-haired, middle-aged, with a sad, lined face; her accent, like his, was that of a Londoner. "We're nearly all of us from up there. That's why we ain't feeling so cheerful just now. What's happened to the fish shop, on the other side, do you know? Bloody Hitler, I'll have his guts for gaiters."

"Garters," Wootton said.

"Smashed to smithereens," Colin answered, rather unkindly. "Not a stone left standing."

"That's where we live," said Wootton, his aggression suddenly evaporating. "Bombed out in London, now bombed out here. By the way, this is my mum. Mum, this is Lockwood. I share his desk at school."

"Oh! Pleased to meet you I'm sure!" She held out her hand for Colin to shake; it seemed quaint, he thought, in such a situation. "Terry's mentioned you. Haven't you, Tel?"

"Yes, Mum." Wootton began to fidget; he was a little embarrassed.

"What did he say?" Colin asked.

"I don't reckon old Kitchen will worry his head too much about the homework now," Wootton said, hastily, so that he could stop his mother from answering. "Eh, Lockwood? He goes mad if work's not in on time; doesn't matter what happened the night before, but . . . well . . . the school might have gone for a burton by now. Hope it has!"

Colin laughed, remembering the Kitchens' arrival at Nimrod's. "I can tell you something about the old fool," he said. What was the point, he asked himself, of keeping on with this silly feud? Terry Wootton's home had been destroyed. He was a decent enough bloke underneath, it seemed. Colin felt sorry for him. He proceeded to relate the evening's experiences, the sherry party, Mrs Wimbleball's performance (he discovered it was very easy to imitate her), his own adventures on the cathedral tower.

Wootton was highly amused by the crushed blackberry and the watery greengage, and so was his mother, though she did say, funny though Colin was, that you shouldn't really be disrespectful to people who weren't there to speak up for themselves; it wasn't proper.

"Reminds me of a raid we had two years back in London, and there was this woman . . ." Wootton launched into a long involved story of New Year's Eve, 1940, of holding a party on the platform of Bethnal Green tube station which was the only place it could be held because of the air-raids, and how some grand lady had become more worried by the bad language than the bombs. She had left at the height of the festivities with a disgusted expression on her face, and had been found, later, fast asleep in the station-cleaners' cupboard.

Mrs Wootton, forgetting that the story wasn't really 'proper', interrupted, took over half the narrative herself, and soon had everybody in the shelter smiling.

By the time the all-clear sounded, Colin had decided Terry Wootton wasn't a bit unpleasant, but almost, if you knew him, someone you wouldn't mind having as a real mate. Why hadn't he discovered this before, he wondered; all that stupid nonsense about evacuees and local yokels: they had all made up their minds, really, to be enemies before they'd found out anything about each other. Neither side had ever given its opponents a chance.

Colin accompanied them up South Street to view the damage. It was exactly as they had feared; there was nothing left of the fish shop, not even one wall. It was impossible to get close because of the flames. Mrs Wootton said she and Terry ought to make their way to Coombe Street where her sister Edie was billeted, and see if they could spend the rest of the night there. Terry pulled a face. "It smells of moth-balls and old women," he protested. "And I'll have to kip down on the carpet."

"We can't exactly park ourselves at the Clarence Hotel!" Mrs Wootton said.

"He can come back to my place if he likes," Colin offered.

After some argument Mrs Wootton agreed, and the two boys set off for Denmark Road, assuring her that they would not get into any mischief. It hadn't occurred to Colin, since he was on the tower, that his own home might have been hit. He was stunned by the sight that greeted him. "Where . . . how . . . Dad! June!" he shouted, panic rising in his voice. "They're in there, Terry, underneath all that lot! What am I going to do?"

He started to run towards the house, but Terry caught up with him and grabbed his arm. "Don't go nuts, Colin! Cool off! There's people digging next door. I'll go over and ask them."

All was well: his father had gone to Nimrod's; June was at the Fosters'. Both were unharmed; they had been in the cupboard under the stairs, and it had stood up, miraculously almost, under the weight of the house collapsing. The Fosters were now in bed; better not disturb them, an air-raid warden advised. The two lads ought to go down to St Leonard's church hall, the nearest rest centre. They could stay the night there, and give their names to whoever was in charge in case they had been listed as missing persons.

"I'm fed up with crowds of people," Terry said, when they were out of earshot. "I'm not going to no rest centre."

"Nor am I. We'll only have a bench or a hard floor to sleep on." Colin gazed up at the front of the house. "I wonder . . . Look, if I could stand on your shoulders, I think I could just get in through my sister's bedroom window."

"What . . . sleep in there? Ain't very safe."

"I didn't mean that. There's a couple of sleeping bags in her cupboard. We could take them and go out in the fields. Find a hay-stack or something. I've always wanted to sleep in a hay-stack."

"Now *that* sounds a bright idea!"

"I think I ought to hang around till Dad comes back, though. Just to see if he's all right."

"He is. The air-raid warden said so."

"Well . . . it's Mum, really. I'm wondering what's happened to her. She should be here by now; I mean the all-clear went ages ago. I know there's a shelter at Nimrod's, but . . . well . . . it's a bit strange."

"Get those sleeping-bags while we're waiting, then. I'll give you a leg-up."

But Colin thought of something easier than standing on

71

Terry's shoulders; in a shed at the bottom of the garden were his father's ladders. He had to scramble over some of the debris to get there, but he managed. The glass in Mary's bedroom window had all been blown out, so climbing inside was no problem. Her room was a jumble of clothes and bedding; the bed itself had been tipped upside down. However, he soon found the sleeping-bags and threw them down to Terry.

"We'd better move sharpish," Terry said. "There'll be trouble if that air-raid warden sees us. I've had dealings with them in London."

"In a minute. We'll be bloody hungry by morning; I'm going to find some food." He returned to the back of the house, and examined the edges of the rubble. Even though the fires of the city centre were some way away, there was light enough to see by. After a little searching he found the frying-pan, three apples, and what he could guess by its smell was the family's entire bacon ration for the week, though it hardly looked like it, being completely smothered in grit and grey dust. On the way back he found a tomato and a jar of salad cream.

"What are you doing?" Terry asked. "The air-raid warden's spotted the ladder. He's coming over."

"I've found our breakfast."

"Come on!"

"I said I wanted to wait for Dad."

"Now then, you two," said the air-raid warden, "I thought I told you to go to the church hall."

"I'm waiting for my mother to come home," Colin said.

"Your father's gone to Nimrod's so he'll have told your mother that the house has been bombed. So she won't be coming here, will she? Now clear off! This building's far from safe, and I want to make sure you two don't climb back inside again." And he started to remove the ladder.

"But she doesn't know where I am! And I don't know if she's been hurt, or anything!"

The air-raid warden considered the problem, and, remembering that Mr Lockwood had said he was going on to the cathedral, suggested that the best thing to do was for the boys to go to the church hall and he would, himself, find Mr Lockwood and tell him Colin was safe. As for his mother, Nimrod's had a perfectly adequate shelter, and even if it had received a direct hit there was no reason to think anyone there had been hurt, let alone killed.

Reassured, they hurried off down the road. Colin stopped at the corner. "I think I'd better leave a message," he said. "I'm sure Mum or Dad will be here sooner or later, and she'll worry even if she's told I'm alive and well." He found the pamphlet on which he'd written down the inscription from General Herbert's monument, and the pencil he'd forgotten to replace on the cathedral bookstall, and scribbled a few lines, saying that he was not at St Leonard's church hall even if she'd heard he was, that he'd obtained a place to sleep for the night, that she wasn't to worry, and he'd see her first thing in the morning. He ran home, and, finding that the air-raid warden had gone, left his note dangling from the letter-box.

Mr Lockwood had not thought to spend long at the cathedral. From a distance it seemed unharmed; he would only look in briefly to check that the firewatchers had put out all the hundreds of incendiaries that must have hit the roof. He had had enough misery and heart-ache for one night. First there had been the sight of Nimrod's, little more than a mountain of smashed stone, glass and tangled metal, then the discovery that Brenda had been taken to hospital; the anxious questions to air-raid wardens and helpers digging in ruined buildings that produced no answers: Colin was missing. For a time he had panicked and run from one group of people to another, asking if his son had been found, then, forcing himself to think rationally and calm down, he had hurried to the hospital, where his relief in finding Mary alive and unharmed and his wife's injuries not as serious as he had feared, was destroyed by the news that Colin had not been brought in with Brenda and Mrs Wimbleball.

It was Lars who convinced him eventually that Colin was probably still alive. Mr Lockwood accidentally met him in the debris in Catherine Street; Lars had been one of the men who had dug the people out of the chaos at Nimrod's. Colin had not been there at the time the bomb had fallen: Lars was absolutely certain of it; he had asked some of the people who had been rescued from the shelter, and Mrs Wimbleball had confirmed it. Colin must have gone to one of the public shelters, and would now be on his way home.

Mr Lockwood decided to return to Denmark Road. The quickest route went past the cathedral, but the scene that met his eyes as he neared the building was totally unexpected: St James's chapel demolished and the roof of the south quire aisle smashed.

The mess was appalling. Already there were many people clearing up, sweeping broken glass and pieces of stone into tidy heaps, others struggling with the larger pieces of masonry. This was no ordinary junk that could be piled on to a lorry and driven off to the nearest tip; it would all have to be carefully sifted, the fragments of precious carving, bits of marble from monuments and tombs, saved and put aside for whenever the building could be properly restored. He went inside and from where the Bishop's throne had once stood he could see the sky, the palace outside, the Bishop's garden: it was little short of a miracle that the whole quire had not collapsed.

The Dean was anxiously inspecting the two pillars of the

quire that had been nearest to the explosion; they were badly cracked and chipped: there was a very real danger that they might have been weakened, the Dean said. The cathedral would have to be closed to visitors until expert opinion had been taken, barriers erected to stop sight-seers coming in through the great hole in the wall. All the windows would have to be boarded up; every single piece of glass had been lost. Services, perhaps, could be held in a chapel well away from the devastation, or on an improvised altar at the west end of the nave. It was of the utmost importance to examine the stability of the towers. If an enemy invasion occurred the bells were not to be rung, for the vibrations might cause further problems. The organ was unplayable, the seventeenth-century casing ripped and torn, the pipes knocked sideways, the keyboard bent out of shape by falling stones. It had stood unchanged for three hundred years, and now look at it! They would have to use Archdeacon Fuller's old harmonium instead.

The Dean insisted that Mr Lockwood should accompany him round the whole building, and scrutinise the rest of the fabric as far as was possible. Mr Lockwood protested, saying that his search for Colin was of more importance, but the Dean silenced him with an icy glare, and a comment to the effect that it would only take five minutes. Five minutes! More like three quarters of an hour, Mr Lockwood thought, but once the Dean had got a bee in his bonnet there was no stopping him. Years of reluctantly falling in with the Dean's whims made Mr Lockwood obey.

The fires outside burned so fiercely that they could see without difficulty. They climbed up the towers to find out if there were any obvious cracks, but there seemed to be no damage at all. "The Normans certainly knew how to build things that last," the Dean observed. They were in the north tower, in the chamber where Great Peter hung in solitary splendour. "Four tons that bell weighs," he said. "And the wood hasn't shifted an inch. And not a mark on the walls either. Incredible." He shone his torch round, for it was darker in here, the only light from outside coming through the louvres that filled the window-spaces. A mysterious black satanic thing Peter looked in the flickering half-light, Mr Lockwood thought. It was the strangest bell of them all: its size was awe-inspiring, almost frightening. Though he had passed by it every week now for years and years, he still had a great respect for it. It had a life of its own, the Peter bell, isolated on the north side, the dark side of the cathedral. It had its own thoughts; standing right underneath it and gazing up into its sombre interior always gave him a sense of alarm. Five hundred years of blackness, of suspension from a beam, and its whole purpose seemed to be to want to crash downwards; it was caught, held, frustrated in that purpose, till one day, if the Dean and chapter neglected it, if death-watch beetle . . .

"We'd better leave," the Dean said. "A proper inspection can be made in the morning. I think the building will hold up for tonight at least."

"I really must go . . . Colin's missing; I think he may be back at home. I – "

"Phone from your office."

"There's not much point; the house has been demolished."

"Phone one of your neighbours, then."

A good idea, Mr Lockwood supposed as he lifted the receiver; the Dean was always full of good ideas that never worked. The telephone would undoubtedly be out of order. But he was surprised to hear the operator say "Number please" almost at once. That, however, was all; before he could ask for John Foster's number there was a jumble of voices on the line through which he could hear a woman say "Exeter operator said 'Office on fire. Excuse errors. Being smoked out.' Hullo, hullo? This is Bristol," and a man replying "We'll have to go soon. Can you get our fire brigade quickly? Eleven of us are trapped." Then, after some indistinct babble, the same man, more urgently: "All exits blocked by fire. Hurry please. Bristol? Bristol!" The voice had a foreign accent; Lars's father, Mr Lockwood guessed. The line went dead.

The Dean came into the office. "I've ordered everybody out of the cathedral," he announced. "Clearing-up can wait till tomorrow. The A.R.P. have just been in; they need men to help dig in the High Street. You'd better be off home. Your son . . . Colin, is it?"

Mr Lockwood needed no second bidding; he ran out of the office.

"June Lockwood!" Pam sat up and rubbed her eyes in amazement. "What on earth are you doing in my bed? Oh, yes. I remember now."

June stirred, muttering something incomprehensible. Then she, too, sat up. "Where am I?" she asked.

"In Heaven," Pam said, stretching her arms. The door opened, and Mrs Foster came in with two cups of tea. She pulled back the curtains: brilliant sunlight, a hot cloudless May morning. "Tea in bed!" Pam exclaimed. "But why? What time is it, Mum?"

"A quarter to ten."

"A quarter to ten! But . . . what about school? Why didn't you wake us up?"

Mrs Foster did not smile. She was tense and weary; last night had completely shattered her nerves. "There isn't a school to go to," she said. "It's been burned out by incendiaries."

77

"Hooray, hooray!" Pam bounced up and down. "How much holiday will there be?"

"I don't know, dear. Not long, I hope."

"Spoilsport!"

"June, dear . . . there's lots of news for you. Now don't get alarmed; it's all right." Mrs Foster sat down by the bed, but her words and her action, unfortunately, made June feel exceedingly alarmed.

"What's wrong? What's wrong?" She sat bolt upright, jogging the tray and spilling the tea.

"Your sister Mary's here. She's fast asleep in our bed; the poor girl's dog-tired after working all night at the hospital. Her boy-friend's on the sofa. He just sat down and fell asleep in the middle of a word. Your brother called, but he's gone off with a friend; said something about fish and chips. I couldn't understand it. June . . . your mother. Nimrod's was bombed. She's in hospital – "

"What!" Pam took her hand and squeezed it.

"She was injured by some shrapnel. It stabbed her just above the hip. It's not serious, but she's feeling a bit weak. Otherwise she's fine, sitting up in bed and drinking orange squash, Mary told me."

"I must go and see her at once!" June threw back the bedclothes.

"June, dear, you can't. The hospital's crowded out with casualties. They won't let any visitors in at the moment. Mary says the corridors look like dormitories, patients lying in rows on the floor. Anyway, your mother will be out soon, tomorrow maybe. You're staying here till then, and so's your father. I don't know about Colin; he was gone before I could mention it. There's no room, really, but he could manage I suppose on a couple of chairs. And Mary's going to sleep at the nurses' hostel

78

for the time being."

"But . . . what will we do about somewhere to live?"

"The cathedral authorities will find another house for you. Mary said your father thinks there might be room in one of those big old mansions in the Close, one where there's just an old clergyman living or something."

June was silent for a while, digesting all this, then she asked, "What about our house? Will it have to be pulled down?"

"I expect so, dear. But there's all sorts of things that can be saved from the front rooms. The neighbours will help move everything for you, and it can all be stored in our garage. Your father's going to organise it as soon as he's had a rest. He was up all night, too." She gazed out of the window. The city centre was still burning.

"Where is he now?"

"Up the road at Mrs Bennett's."

"What happened to Miss Chadwick?"

"She died, love."

Mrs Foster went downstairs. The two girls stared up at the ceiling. There were cracks in it, patterns like a map of a railway system, that had not been there a day ago.

"Oh well," said Pam. "It could be worse."

"Yes. But I've lost all my books and my toys. And my clothes. It's like . . . having to be born again."

"Born again! You do talk rubbish, June! There'll be compensation, won't there? From the government. You can have a lovely shopping spree. Think of it! Buying new dresses, and card games, and – "

"Are there any shops left, though? And you need coupons for new clothes."

"I expect your mum's got enough. I'll come with you and help."

79

"I suppose you're right; it could be worse. But poor Miss Chadwick!"

"She was a funny old creature. Dad said she must be nearly eighty. That's old!"

"Seventy-two, in fact."

"She bought me an ice-cream once. Before the war."

"When Colin accidentally knocked balls and shuttlecocks over the fence she'd always throw them back. And say they hadn't really damaged the bluebells, well only just a little bit . . . I liked her. She was nice."

"Yes. She was."

June burst into tears; she wasn't sure why, but once started, she couldn't stop. She buried her face in the pillow and howled. Pam seemed to be affected too; she started snivelling, then turned away and cried her eyes out.

Colin woke, bewildered for a moment by the light, the absence of curtains, the sweet dusty smell of hay. He turned his head. Terry was already awake, sitting up and chewing a piece of straw. "This is good," said Colin, scratching himself. "Never slept better in all my life. Lying in a sleeping-bag with nothing on . . . it's a lovely sensation."

"Breakfast," said Terry. "My stomach's got a different kind of sensation. How are we going to cook that bloody bacon? It's filthy."

"Pick all the bits of dirt off first. You'll see. Country boy will reveal all." He struggled out of the sleeping-bag and put his clothes on. Terry sniggered. "What's so funny?"

"Nothing."

"Follow me, then." He climbed down the ladder and went outside into the field. The sun was warm on his skin. But he would love a bath, he thought; hay tickled, and it was full of insects. He began to collect twigs so that he could build a fire. Terry appeared, yawning. "Bring some straw," Colin said. "Oh, God! We haven't any matches."

"I've got some."

"Why? For cigarettes?"

"Yes. Do you want one?"

"Not now."

After they had eaten they smoked a cigarette each; it was only the third time Colin had done so and it made his head spin. It was marvellously peaceful out here in the fields, almost unnaturally so, he thought. The blue sky, the warmth, the view across to Haldon and its tower: he was afraid it would prove to be a dream and he would awake to the chaos and darkness of last night. Ever since he had woken the blitz had been in his head, the flames, the acrid smoke, buildings disintegrating: but particularly the multitude of terrifying noises, the mad scream of planes diving, explosions, the roar, something like a cross between thunder and a colossal waterfall, of collapsing masonry, the rattle of machine-gun bullets. Here there was only the drone of insects and a distant blackbird singing. It seemed quite unreal, almost as if he himself was not part of the experience, for if this was reality, then the air-raid was a nightmare that belonged to a different person, a different Colin. Absurd, he told himself; the cigarette was making his mind play tricks. He must go back to the city at once and find his family. His mother would undoubtedly need pacifying, and Dad would want him to help salvage their possessions, those that were still intact, from their house. Dad: suppose the air-raid warden had *not* found him last night? That possibility filled him with horror; why had he not thought of it before?

"Come on," he said, scrambling to his feet. "We must go home."

"Yes," Terry answered. His mind seemed to be on the same subject. "My mum will be worrying too."

On the way back, Colin said "You're not a bad cook, Terry." He was still thinking of Dad not knowing his son was alive and safe, and the idea made him feel so uncomfortable that conversation on any subject seemed preferable.

"Had to. Since Dad died."

Colin grunted, and stared at him. "Didn't know he was dead. What happened?"

"Killed at Dunkirk." He squinted up at the sky, shielding his eyes with his hand.

"I'm thirsty. My throat feels like the back end of a cow."

"Who owns that barn, the one where we slept?"

"I don't know. Some farmer."

"Look . . . I've just had an idea. You give it me, when you said I wasn't a bad cook."

"What is it?"

"A *very* good idea! Come up to the fish shop, what's left of it that is, soon as you're free."

Six

THERE WAS nothing for Mrs Lockwood to do but worry. It was the one thing everybody, including the doctors, had said she must not do, but it was quite impossible to avoid it. The house had been destroyed, and though Ron had told her that an amazing number of their possessions had been saved — the Fosters' garage was so full, he said, that he didn't know where to put half the stuff — she knew very well that he was just trying to cheer her up. He was always over-confident, the eternal optimist; it was her role in the family to see the problems, to examine things realistically. He and June, she had to admit, would be well looked after at the Fosters', but she longed to hug her younger daughter and have a long talk, a good cry: all the family had been in to see her, it was true — Mary had broken the rules and smuggled them in — but they were not allowed to stay for more than a few minutes in case there was trouble. And there was a strained and artificial atmosphere at the best of times about hospital visits; even one's nearest and dearest were never their real selves, all trying desperately to think of something cheerful to say to the patient and failing to sound as if they had any conviction whatsoever.

Colin was the chief problem. That boy needed constant nagging if he was ever to maintain a minimum standard of civilised behaviour. Coming in here, that smart expensive suit torn to shreds (she knew he couldn't help that, but the annoying thing was he didn't seem to care), and his appearance utterly filthy; refusing to stay at the Fosters', preferring to sleep in a barn! The idea! If left to himself her son would become a tramp. And Ron was no help at all. All he could think of was his cathedral, and finding a new home for the family — well, she could hardly blame him for doing that, she supposed — but he ought to insist on Colin being washed and properly fed and clothed, sent to school, and given a bed to sleep in somewhere. What would happen if there was another raid tonight! Colin might be out roaming the streets in Heaven knew what company; he might even be killed. Of course the school had been damaged a little, but he should be down there, finding out where to go and what to do; she was certain, though he hadn't actually said so, that the school was the one place in Exeter which he was avoiding like the plague. "Oh, let him alone!" Ron said. "There's not much harm he can come to. He's looking after himself for once, and enjoying it too. Learning a few things about life." Learning! There were times when she thought her husband deserved to be carted off to Digby and have his brains carefully examined.

She told Colin that Mr and Mrs Kitchen had died. Rather to her surprise he seemed very upset. He had always given the impression that the history master was worse than Hitler.

"I'll never be able to show him this." He pulled a dirty old piece of stone out of his pocket.

"What is it?"

"Just something I found. Some ancient thing." He sat down on the end of the bed, unusually pale beneath the grime on his face. He was really shaken, almost in tears. "He was a good teacher. He really did know how to teach. Why him?"

"But you used to say –"

"I know what I used to say!" He sounded so angry and scowled so fiercely at her that she decided to change the subject. She would never understand him, she said. What on earth was he doing on the top of the south tower of the cathedral during an air-raid? He could have been blown to bits. Had he no sense? He just shrugged his shoulders, and sat, hunched and silent, lost in sorrow. One day he would do something quite mad, she thought; and yet – it was not even twenty-four hours ago – he had been so polite to the Nimrod customers, so deft with the sherry bottles and the refreshments: he could be well-mannered if he wanted to; he could follow all the normal observances.

"Bye, Mum. See you." He got up and left hurriedly.

"Colin!" But he did not stop, did not even turn his head.

Mary came through the ward. "I can't stay now," she said, "but I'll be back in a moment. Are you all right?"

"I'm fine."

"Anything you want?"

"No."

"Don't look so down-hearted, Mum. Nothing's as bad as it seems."

Her elder daughter worried her too. If Mary didn't have a few hours off soon she would knock herself up completely. Her face was pale and spotty, and an enormous tiredness showed in her eyes. Of course there had been an emergency; the nurses were rushed off their feet, but it was no use working themselves to a standstill as Mary did. She'd end up in a hospital bed herself. Mrs Lockwood had mentioned it earlier to Lars, when he popped in for a moment, but he had only looked embarrassed and said it was none of his business. Mary and Lars: that wouldn't come to anything; she knew that. Mary was in love with him; it was obvious and she couldn't disguise it, even though she tried to. But there was nothing on his side. Mary hadn't discussed it with her; she never did say much, but, well, women, Mrs Lockwood knew from long experience, had intuitions about these things, intuitions that were invariably right. She didn't blame Lars, naturally; how could he permit himself to think of anything like that when he was due to leave . . . tomorrow, wasn't it? But falling in love, she reflected, occurred at the oddest times and obeyed no laws; it certainly wouldn't be influenced by the thought of going out to fight in Africa or somewhere next week. She recalled the first time she'd met Ron; she'd thought him a complete drip, a total non-entity, standing glum and conversationless on the edge of a tennis club dance, his hands in his pockets, and, well, look what had happened!

What was the matter, she wondered; this bad mood was not like her usual self. She felt weak and depressed; the reason was, she supposed, that she had lost a great deal of blood, and there were so many bandages swathed round her that she could hardly move. She couldn't remember much about what had happened; it was so dark: there was just this terrifying noise and a sense of the world falling apart (squashed in, she thought, would have been more appropriate, but things disintegrating, flying outwards from the centre was the feeling), then nothing more. Nothing, until she had come round in this ward, aching dully all over, limp, tearful, unable to cope with anything. Just rest, eat and drink, the doctor had ordered; she could probably leave tomorrow. Normally they would keep her in hospital for a week, but there was a great shortage of beds and the staff were stretched to the limits of their endurance. The less badly injured would have to go home as soon as they could. Home? There was no such place now.

"Brenda! Why are you looking so gloomy?" Lorna Wimbleball, in the next bed, had just woken up. What a remarkable woman she was! What energy, what courage! But somewhat overwhelming when one was feeling shaky and depressed. The wooden beam that had split the lift open, and, in doing so, saved their lives, had crushed her legs. The doctors had thought at first they would have to amputate. But further examination had shown this would not be necessary, and now her legs were encased in plaster, pointing upwards at an angle of forty-five degrees on some peculiar system of wires and pulleys. It must be very painful, Mrs Lockwood thought, the blood being prevented from circulating properly, but Mrs Wimbleball said she couldn't feel a thing; it was as if she had no legs at all.

"Daphne came while you were asleep. How everyone contrives to sneak in here when visitors aren't allowed I can't imagine! Anyway, she's brought your film."

"*Has* she! Oh, the dear!" Mrs Wimbleball turned and looked at the precious can, perched on the table by her bed. "I don't think I can reach it."

"Daphne said she'd run it through, and there's not a mark on it. Amazing!"

"That's super! Absolutely super! Brenda! I've just had a brainwave! If we could persuade your little daughter who's been so kind and so attentive –"

"June?" Mrs Lockwood asked, bewildered.

"No, no, Brenda, the little nurse one, Miriam."

"Mary."

"Yes. Mary." She paused. "What was I going to say about her? I've completely forgotten! My memory seems to have got stuck in that *ghastly* lift-shaft! Oh yes. If she could somehow rustle up a decent projector, better than my wretched old thing, we could go on with the show in here! What do you think of that?" Nimrod autumn fashions could not have been further from Mrs Lockwood's mind at that moment, and the thought of Lorna Wimbleball going through her routine in a hospital ward, in which not one of the patients as far as she could tell had ever set foot in the shop, made her feel very uneasy. So she smiled blankly, and said nothing. "Oh I know we don't have our usual clientèle here, but does that matter? With a *war* on? It would do all these good people" – she waved her arm in a gesture that embraced the entire room – "a world of good to see some elegant clothes. Don't you think?"

"Er . . . yes."

"Splendid. That's settled. As soon as Miriam –"

"Mary."

"– comes back, I'll ask her to arrange everything." She was silent for a moment, then said "It's fearfully tiresome that my projector wasn't scrunched to atoms."

"Why?"

"If it was then Nimrod would just simply have to buy me a decent one! Do you know, by the way, if head office *realises* I'm in here, strung up to the ceiling like meat in a pork butcher's? Heavens! They'll have a fit! Has Daphne informed them?"

"I didn't think to ask her."

"Well, when she next comes in I'll have to dictate a memo. The inconvenience! *Sod* those ghastly Nazis! Excuse me, Brenda, but there are times when one simply *has* to use words like that. I just hope our boys give them back as good as they gave us."

"I couldn't agree with you more."

At that moment the door opened and Ron Lockwood burst in, looking very excited. He seized his wife's hands. "We've got a house!" he said. "It's all settled! Canon Brinkworth's place in Cathedral Close. Oh, it's a beautiful old house, Brenda. Huge! He had evacuees, but they moved out last week and went back to Liverpool. Isn't that a stroke of luck? Of course we won't have the whole of it; the Canon's still living there. But the upstairs is ours, two floors, virtually a self-contained flat!"

"A flat, Ron! Do you think that's wise? Colin and June in a flat! How will they get on with the Canon?"

"Oh, he's old and very deaf and won't hear a sound. I'm moving our things over there in the morning."

Mary came in. "Miriam!" Mrs Wimbleball cried. "*Do* come here, please! I want to ask you a favour!"

Terry wanted to try and rescue the fish from the cellar of his mother's shop. It was stored there in a freezer; if it was left it would go off rapidly, as the city's power supply was out of action. The cellar, he thought, would be undamaged: his idea was to cook the fish and offer it to any passer-by who, owing to the lack of electricity and gas, was unable to get anything to eat.

The shop was a charred ruin, and the first job was to shift a mountain of bricks, wood, and glass. It took hours of hard work. The fire had burned itself out, but some pieces of wood were still smouldering, and many of the bricks were so hot that they scorched their hands touching them. Colin requisitioned a broom which was lying on the pavement, and after they had cleared sufficient space in the wreckage, he swept all the smaller bits of rubbish out into the gutter. Then he heaped sticks and paper on to an improvised grate of broken stones, while Terry went downstairs for the fish. Slimy wet boxes of cod, hake, and a few precious pieces of plaice: the ground floor of the shop had held firm when the rest of the building had fallen, and the cellar looked much as it usually did, apart from thick layers of dust and plaster over everything.

"Might as well do the spuds," Terry said, dragging a sack of potatoes up the steps. "Can't chip them of course. The fish fryer's blown to bits. We'll poke them in the fire and roast them in their jackets."

"We need more than one frying-pan," Colin said.

"Go and see what you can scrounge." While he was away, Terry found a large piece of cardboard, and wrote out a sign that read: "T. WOOTTON AND C. LOCKWOOD. Noted friers of quality fish. Business as usual. Hot meals on sale FREE!"

Colin re-appeared after a while with a frying-pan, larger than the one they already had, and five pounds of lard. "Where did you pinch that?" Terry asked, admiringly. "You local yokels are as good at nicking stuff as us evacuees. Better, in fact."

"The grocer down the street gave it me. He was trying to see what was left of his shop, and I asked him if he had a spare frying-pan. What did I need it for, he wanted to know. When I told him he laughed and gave me this – it's a bit battered; blown out into the yard last night, he said – and all this cooking fat. He says there's plenty more we can have if we run out. Yes, and he'll be down with his family in twenty minutes for something to eat. They're all starving, he says. So our first order's cod and spuds for two and plaice and spuds for three."

"Right. We'd better get going, then." Terry, very business-like, started to put the fish in the pans, and Colin lit the fire.

"They'll have to eat with their fingers," Colin said. "We've got no plates, no knives and forks. How are we going to keep the food hot?"

"Put it on some of those bricks over there. We burned our hands on them, didn't we? They'll be just the job."

Mrs Wootton appeared. "What the hell do you two think you're up to?" she demanded, amazed at the sight of her son frying fish in the middle of a bombed ruin.

"Business as usual, Mum. Says so on that notice."

"But you can't do that!"

"Why not?"

Mrs Wootton couldn't think of any good reason why not. After considering the matter for some moments, she said "I don't know, I'm sure. You're a caution, Tel, and no mistake. Do you want some help?"

"Nope."

"In that case, then, if I'm not wanted, I'll leave you to it. Plenty to do at Edie's, there is. Whatever will you think of next?"

"Flying to the moon."

"You'd both better come down to Edie's when you've got a free moment and have a bath."

"O.K. Mum."

A bath, Colin thought, would be marvellous. But if they were going to take time off he ought to go to the hospital and see his mother. There was no hurry about that, however; she was very comfortable, Mrs Foster had said, and she would probably be horrified if she knew what he was up to. There was no point in her being horrified, but he was sure, somehow, that she would be, and would stop him, confined though she was to her bed, from returning to the fish-frying. She had an astonishing power to stop him doing things; nobody else could. He had already made up his mind not to introduce her to Terry. Not a suitable friend she would say, too coarse and rough. Bound to lead him into trouble. He salved his conscience by deciding that she was in no fit state to be worried about him. She might even have a relapse.

"Mmm! That cod smells good!" said Mrs Wootton. "Can I have a bit?"

"Sorry, Mum. It's for Mr Muir and his family. Come back in

91

ten minutes."

"All right, I will. And I'll bring you up a pot of tea. Are you thirsty?"

"You bet we are."

"Edie's got some cakes. Home-made. I'll bring them up as well; you both deserve it. And if I see the Mayor I'll tell him you're feeding the five thousand and deserve the bloody V.C."

Business, at first, was quiet, but word soon got round, and although a few people just came to stare, or give them dark suspicious looks, there were others who were genuinely hungry and very grateful to receive a piece of fried fish and a roast potato. Soon things got quite hectic. Terry did all the frying; Colin organized the roasting: his hands were now so thick with dirt that he scarcely noticed how hot a potato was when he raked it out of the fire. By mid-afternoon they had served forty-three fish dinners.

Colin had less work to do than Terry, and he spent his spare time dragging away more of the bricks and building a little shelter with them. A rusty piece of corrugated iron, wedged down with stones, furnished the roof.

"What's it for?" Terry asked.

"I thought we might sleep here tonight if we felt like it. On the premises. I'll scout round later and find a mattress or two. There's sure to be some old bedding somewhere that didn't get burnt." He gazed over the whole devastated area, Market Street, most of South Street, George Street, Milk Street, the top of Fore Street: in the middle of all that, he was sure, there had once been a furniture shop. That was the place to look for mattresses.

At tea-time he went to see his mother, and came back depressed and sad. He threw the piece of marble on to the ground. "No point in showing that to old Kitchen now," he said to Terry. "He died last night."

"What!"

"He *and* his wife. They were at Nimrod's, but didn't get into the shelter in time. Poor bastards." He sat down in the rubble, resting his head on his knees.

Terry fiddled about with the frying-pan, not knowing what to say. "Where *did* you get this?" He picked up Paul Sanders, mason, and looked at it curiously.

"In the cathedral."

Terry wiped it carefully on his trousers, and gave it back to Colin. "I should look after him if I was you, your great-great-whatsit-grandfather."

"I don't want it now."

"Don't be stupid." Colin took it from him. "It's been all go while you were at the hospital. A man who'd had a piece of hake this morning came in just now with some breadcrumbs. Mr Muir's been along with some more fat. And old Mrs Webster, she runs the chippie in Summerland Street, she's bombed out too. She says she's got some more fish when ours packs up. So we can go on doing this tomorrow."

"Oh no you can't," said a voice. It was Mr Lockwood. "I've got us a new house, in Cathedral Close, and I need your help, Colin, to move the furniture first thing in the morning, what's left of it. I'm on my way to tell your mother. So you're now a fishmonger, are you! I'll have cod and chips, please, while I'm here."

"No chips, Dad. Only roast potatoes."

"Roast potatoes will do very well."

"Potat*o*. In the singular. They're rationed."

Music suddenly started to blare from a loudspeaker on the other side of the road. Mr Cousins, the draper, was standing in the remains of his shop, playing a gramophone record of "Land

93

of Hope and Glory". An enormous Union Jack fluttered proudly from his one surviving window-frame. People stopped; soon a small crowd gathered. They began to sing. When the record had finished Mr Cousins put it on again, and came out on to the pavement, waving his arms about, conducting.

Land of hope and glory, mother of the free,
How shall we extol thee, who art born of thee?
Wider still and wider shall thy bounds be set;
God who made thee mighty, make thee mightier yet!
God who made thee mighty, make thee mightier yet!

"Elgar's brass," said Mr Lockwood. "It never fails."

Women were unashamedly weeping. "That's right!" a man yelled out. "Mother of the free! Free, that's what we are, aren't we? Let them have it back, that's what I say, just like they handed it to us last night! Blast them to pieces!" There were cheers and shouts of agreement from the crowd, applause. Mr Cousins then played "Rule Britannia", "Jerusalem", and "God Save the King". Colin found many of the well-worn familiar phrases now stirred him deeply; the blitz had given them a new importance: "Blest isle with matchless, with matchless beauty crowned," "Britons never never never shall be slaves!", "Till we have built Jerusalem in England's green and pleasant land", "Send him victorious, happy and glorious". The emotion made him shiver; his mouth trembled and his eyes were wet.

"A wild chauvinist orgy," Mr Lockwood murmured, half captivated, half disliking the feelings aroused.

"What's that mean, Dad?" Colin asked, blowing his nose.

"Admirable patriotism. Or ugly nationalism, according to

94

your point of view."

"I know what my point of view is."

"Remember the Germans have their own songs. Exact equivalents."

After "The King" there was silence. People stood still for a moment, hoping for more, then, as if they were coming out of a trance, they began to move away. Mr Cousins returned to the task of seeing if there was anything he could salvage from his shop. Some of the crowd crossed the road and a small queue formed, waiting for fried fish.

"I must get busy, Dad," Colin said.

"Are you going back to your hay-loft tonight?"

"No, we're staying here in the shop."

"Shop?" Mr Lockwood looked at the ruins. "Oh, I see."

"There's mattresses somewhere, and I took the sleeping-bags from the cupboard in Mary's bedroom."

"So that's why the ladder's lying on the grass! I did wonder if we'd been visited by a burglar. Well, I suppose you were a burglar, weren't you? Looting. Now, Colin. Enough's enough. There's a bed for you in Cathedral Close as from tomorrow night, and I shall want to see you in it. Is that clear?"

"Yes, Dad."

"Your mother's already worried sick about you, and I want her out of that hospital sane in mind as well as body. Understand?"

"Yes, Dad."

Some time later Mr Cousins came over and asked for two pieces of cod and two roast potatoes. He apologised for wanting a double portion, but he hadn't eaten all day, he said. He then gave Colin and Terry a ten-shilling note each. The food was free, they protested, but Mr Cousins was adamant. They had both shown initiative, devotion to duty, loyalty to the com-

95

munity, and a lot of other things like that, in these cataclysmic times; their fried fish had boosted the morale of the citizens in a way that could not possibly be measured. He had been in the trenches in the Great War, and knew what was what. They deserved the money; if he could spare more he would have made it a pound each. And if he ran into the Mayor — a personal friend of his — he would tell him there were at least two specimens of English youth in this great and glorious city that were of the same breed that had made Britannia rule the waves.

"Between him and your mother," Colin said, when he had gone, "we shall be in the King's Birthday Honours list in next to no time. What a peculiar man! What shall we do with it?"

"The money? Buy beer and fags."

"With *all* of it?"

"Well, maybe not quite all. But we'll have to close now anyway; we've run out of fish. I reckon we've earned ourselves a drink, don't you?"

"Yes."

"Ninety-seven fish dinners we've served today. I think that's a record for Wootton's, either in Bethnal Green or Exeter, Wootton and Lockwood as it now is. I'll have to check up with Mum."

"They won't serve us in a pub, Terry. We're under age."

"Oh-ho, now here's where the Cockneys'll teach you yokels a thing or two. I go into the off-licence part, see, and say it's for my mum. It usually works."

"I bet it doesn't. Which pub are you going to try?"

"The Turk's Head's still upright and so's the White Hart. They're nearest. Bit too snooty, though. The Elephant in North Street, I'll go there. Scruffy old hole."

While Terry was away Colin took down the sign advertising hot meals on sale, free, and generally tidied up the ruins. It was getting dark. He threw more wood on the fire in case the night turned cold.

"Three pints each," Terry said, returning with an armful of bottles. "And twenty Weights. No bother, son, it was, no bother at all." He looked very pleased with himself. "If my mum comes up, hide it quick. I don't think somehow she'd be that happy."

They pulled their mattresses up to the fire, and, though it was not late, bedded down in their sleeping-bags. They smoked and drank and talked for hours. Three lots of visitors interrupted them: June, Pam and Mrs Foster were the first; they had come down to inspect the sea-food restaurant, as Mrs Foster called it, a special treat before the girls went to bed. Then Mrs Wootton arrived, and tried to persuade Terry to spend the night at his aunt's. Ah, but that would leave Colin on his own, Terry argued, and Colin's father hadn't minded him sleeping out. Mrs Wootton wavered, then made them promise that if it rained or if the air-raid warning went they would go at once to Holy Trinity shelter. "At least," she conceded, "you look cosy, and Edie's only got the carpet." Finally, Lars and Mary appeared; the fame of the fried fish had reached the hospital, she said, and they'd come to see for themselves. A pity there was no frying tonight; she was hungry, but not to worry: she wouldn't be poisoned now by Colin's cooking. Get lost you old bag, he said, and Lars, as they went, remarked rather sarcastically that he thought it was a fish and chip shop they were supposed to be operating, not a brewery.

"I thought we'd got the bottles out of the way rather well," Colin said, as he wriggled down inside his sleeping-bag. "On all three occasions. And neatly dropped our fags into the fire, too. How did he know?"

"Smelled our breath, I reckon."

At about half past eleven they both felt sleepy, and the conversation petered out. Colin had heard what it was like to grow up in the East End – the little Jewish food-shops, trips to Canvey Island, communists and fascists fighting each other, gang warfare, the London blitz, a school where if you weren't prepared to stand up for yourself and hit back from the day you started till the day you left then you'd sink without trace. It made his own life seem very tame, but Terry evidently didn't think so: he listened to everything Colin had to say about fishing in the Exe, surfing in a rough sea on the north coast, camping on Dartmoor, Nimrod's, the cathedral, placid country kids, and said it all sounded a lot nicer than Bethnal Green.

The day's hard work, the beer, Terry: I'm happy, Colin said to himself, and the sensation did not vanish when he repeated the words. Could it be better? Yes, he found himself thinking, but it took him some while to find the reason, and, when he did, he was extremely surprised at the way his mind had worked, because he had never thought it in his life before. It must be this grown-up living, he decided, doing what he pleased all day long, and adults like his father not objecting . . . It would be good to have a girl-friend in a sleeping-bag beside him. "Do you know many girls, Terry?" he asked.

"Dozens."

"Honestly?"

"Yes. How about you?"

"Three or four." Pictures of June's giggling cronies, and Mary's soppy crowd came into his head. Were there no other girls he knew, real girls? There weren't. "Is there . . . someone special? I mean, do you have a girl-friend?"

"No." Colin was relieved to hear this. "Do you?"

"No."

"Well," said Terry, turning over and trying to make himself

comfortable, "it's about time we both did, don't you reckon?"

"Yes. Yes, I do."

"If the brains of us two can feed half the city on fried fish, then they can easily sort out a pair of likely females." He yawned. "I can't stay awake no longer."

"Same here."

"See you, then. 'Goodnight, sweet repose, all the bed and half the clothes.' Mum sometimes said that."

"Mine used to say 'To bed, to bed says Sleepy-head; tarry awhile says Slow. Open the book says the wise old Rook; we'll have some prayers before we go.'"

"That sounds potty."

Colin laughed. "Goodnight."

"Goodnight."

Seven

IT WAS not like home. What annoyed June most was being unable to find where anything had been put; her slippers had
disappeared completely, and even something as large as the
lounge hearth-rug was only revealed after a long search. It was
under a cardboard box containing Dad's vests and Mary's hats:
someone, Colin presumably, had dumped the whole lot in the
bath and piled coats and cushions on top. And there was Canon
Brinkworth. Not that he was unfriendly or frightening; in fact
he was rather a sweet old man who smelled of snuff and spoke in
a quavering grandfather voice: the problem was, simply, that he
was there. It meant not making too much noise in case he was
disturbed, and it meant being unable to live downstairs. She felt
insecure: she couldn't slam the front door and shut the whole
world out as in Denmark Road; she couldn't say this is *my* house
and I can do what I like in it. But, she supposed, she would have
to get used to it. There was, for the present, no alternative.

Mary was now going to live permanently in the nurses'
hostel, so it didn't matter that there were only three bedrooms.
But Mary had been lucky. All her possessions had survived the
explosion apart from her china ornaments – a collection of hideous miniature horses – whereas June had lost everything, toys,
books, bed, bedding, pictures: nothing remained except the

clothes she had been wearing when the bomb fell. Colin, too, had only his ruined best suit and the jacket he had left on top of the cathedral tower. He didn't mind, but she did. The thought of her little room at Denmark Road brought a lump to her throat: the row of dolls on their shelf, the old wardrobe and the chest of drawers, her pink eiderdown, her bookcase with its Enid Blytons and Arthur Ransomes, all gone forever. She loved her things; she loved re-arranging them, making them neat and pretty. That pink eiderdown had kept her warm at night for as long as she could remember.

This bedroom here was certainly on a grander scale. It had big windows with seats and great sweeping curtains like in a theatre; there were two built-in cupboards, and a massive black beam right across the ceiling. It looked out on to the lawn in front of the cathedral; she could sit up here and watch the people walking past, and the morning sun would dazzle on the cathedral walls. There had been no argument with Colin about it; he had willingly accepted the tiny attic at the back of the house for himself. There was just enough space in it for a mattress and nothing else, and it stared straight into an ugly blank wall. But Colin seemed indifferent, not even caring that he had no proper bed for the moment, only the mattress and a sleeping-bag. At least she had Mary's bed, her little table, her bookcase. Maybe that was the trouble: Mary's things looked so pathetic in this huge empty room.

The door opened and Dad came in. "We'll buy you some pictures on Saturday," he said, "and some clothes if we've got enough coupons. And you can choose some new toys. So cheer up."

"How did you know I was feeling miserable?"

Mr Lockwood smiled. "Look at your face in the mirror."

"The bomb smashed it."

"Which? The face or the mirror?" She said nothing. "June! That's not my happy uncomplicated daughter! I'll buy you a new mirror."

"I'm sorry, Dad."

"June, love . . ."

"I know. I know."

"I've begged and borrowed from everybody, and we've just about got a home together. Plates, cups, saucepans, cutlery, even some chairs and a table. We can live all right. The lounge furniture's here; it wasn't touched, well, scratched a bit, that's all. I suppose your bedroom isn't quite what it should be, but Colin's only got a mattress, remember."

"Yes. I'm sorry."

"Let's go out, shall we? There's something rather important we must do."

"What's that?" She gazed out of the window, thinking about her dolls, the old smashed ones, the new ones she would like.

"See if you can guess. No? Well, the city's getting back to normal. The electricity and gas and water are all working now. A lot of the debris has been cleared and you can drive through some of the streets. A few buses are running. You both have to go back to school tomorrow – "

"Tomorrow? Where?" She rather liked the idea of school: at least it would be something she was used to, a part of the familiar routine restored.

"A big house in Spicer Road. Number twelve. I met Miss Martin earlier and she wants the children there at nine o'clock sharp. The council are sending spare desks and books and blackboards. Colin's school was hardly damaged at all; he was meant to be there today and yesterday. His little holiday ends in a few hours' time."

"He's worked jolly hard, moving cart-loads of furniture."

102

"Quite true, my love. And this evening he can have a bath and go to bed early. And sleep in this house. And tomorrow morning he can be at school at nine o'clock sharp too. He won't like it I don't doubt, but ordinary life has to go on. I've even got a promise of a second-hand uniform for him."

"He certainly won't like *that*! He was really pleased to find his cap and tie and blazer torn to shreds!"

"I daresay. Mr Alderdyce's grandson left last year, and they've still got his uniform. Colin can go round and collect it later."

"Dad . . . what's this important thing we must do now?"

"Guess. Colin will be here in a moment. He's bringing the last cart-load of stuff; we'll have moved everything in. Our new home will be complete, won't it?"

He was smiling to himself; was it a surprise, she wondered, some little mystery he had invented to please her, to take her mind off things?

"Complete?" she said. "Yes, I suppose so."

"There's something missing. What is it?"

June sighed wearily. "Oh, Dad, I don't know. Honestly I don't."

He laughed. "Mum."

"Oh!" Her hand flew to her mouth. "How could I forget? Oh, Dad, don't tell her!"

"Of course not. And we're going to fetch her now."

"Now? This minute?"

"Come on." He held his hand out to her. "I can hear Colin downstairs. We'll all go. The long way round, by Catherine Street; I want to get some tobacco."

There was indeed a bus, June noticed, and the shops that had escaped or were only slightly damaged were open for business; people were buying toothpaste and apples and bread just as they usually did. But St Catherine's church and the Country Inn no longer existed. A street-lamp was bent over at an absurd angle, twisted, like a stick of liquorice. Workmen were shovelling rubble on to lorries in Bedford Circus. All the houses there were either smashed to bits or roofless, windowless ruins, charred and blackened. The walls were being pulled down by squads of men in helmets, one house after another. Soon it would be a huge empty desert.

But tomorrow there was school. That gave her a warm comforting feeling. There would be all sorts of stories to listen to from her friends, what had happened to them during that dreadful night. And she had a story herself, of course, the cupboard under the stairs, then crawling out through the wreckage. She hoped fervently that everybody would be there, no-one dead or in hospital. It would be terrible if . . . but now there was Mum to bring home. Oh, it would be good to see her walking about; it wouldn't even matter being scolded or shouted at, just so long as she was back home! She skipped and jumped, and ran down the street.

But Mrs Lockwood, though she was dressed and ready, was not able to leave immediately. Patients from other parts of the hospital, sitting on the ends of beds or in wheel-chairs, filled the ward, and half a dozen nurses had taken time off to watch. Two young women in hats and overcoats stared from a film screen: Mrs Wimbleball was in mid-performance; Nimrod's autumn collection, part two.

"This is Irene and Noreen; yes, the names do sound hilarious I know, but what *magic* those hats are! Just because there's a war on there's no need to look drab. Daphne ran those hats up herself out of the cheapest material you could possibly imagine, dyed them a sort of hectic plum, and don't they look *heavenly*?

We're selling them for only **three and** six. And do look at Noreen's shoes! I shouldn't say so myself, but I painted those gold lines. You know, there's an awful lot of nonsense talked about gold paint these days. I bought a sixpenny pot from Woolworth's and just splashed it on!"

Colin, who was standing at the back, knew he was going to laugh again. He could feel it beginning to simmer and bubble inside him, like a spring of water that has to force its way up through the earth. No amount of glaring from his mother, who was sitting on a chair beside him, could suppress it. But a conversation between Mary and another nurse shocked him like an unexpected slap in the face, and, suddenly, there was no more humour to be found in Mrs Wimbleball's monologue; it was the sad, brave façade of a woman whose existence might be, from now on, tragic and futile.

"Isn't she a scream!" Mary's friend whispered.

"You wouldn't think so if you knew what I heard today," said Mary.

"What's that?"

"Her legs are paralysed, Shirley. Doctor Pepper says there's almost no chance of her being able to walk again. She can move her arms and head, yes, and bend at the waist, and the bones will set all right, but the nervous system's severed. She may have to spend the rest of her life in a wheel-chair. She knows it, too; I think she knew before the doctors confirmed it. She's got no-one, no children, no husband. Divorced, apparently. This is her last fashion show for Nimrod."

Colin, horrified, tried to imagine what it would be like not to play any games, swim, climb cliffs, go fishing, be totally incapable of movement, unable to twitch a muscle. He would rather be dead, he thought. The boredom! The nuisance to friends and relatives! It would be quite intolerable.

"I wonder," Shirley said. "She's a very determined lady. Some people overcome difficulties worse than that."

"You may be right," Mary answered. "I wouldn't like to have to try, though."

"Nor me. But I don't think it will be her last fashion show. I wouldn't bet on it anyway." She glanced at the picture on the screen, and said "Awful hats, aren't they? I don't think Lars would fancy you in one of those. How's his father? Was he badly burned?"

"One hand is. Otherwise he's all right."

"It wasn't much fun at the telephone exchange, so I'm told."

"Everyone got out alive. But some of the burns are very serious."

Colin stared at Mrs Wimbleball. She was immobile, except for her head, vigorous and bright-eyed, and her left arm, which waved majestically at the screen. "Last picture, darlings. A little something to remind us all that better times are just round the corner. Yes, the latest thing in evening wear. I shouldn't advise it in an air-raid shelter, but when the lights go on again and there are parties being held all over the world, this will make you look *ravishing! Isn't* it lovely! All the colours of the rainbow, and doesn't it flow! And I must let you all into a little secret. It costs next to nothing, because it's made of dishcloths!" An amazed silence greeted this. "Dyed, of course." There was another pause, then "Lights, Daphne darling!" It was over; the curtains were drawn back and daylight flooded into the room. Nurses bustled about; people walked down the ward, through the doorway. Mrs Wimbleball lay still.

Mary returned to the house in Cathedral Close with the rest of the family; it was the first time since before the air-raid that they had all been together on their own. They watched in

106

silence as Mrs Lockwood examined the living room, opened drawers and cupboards in the kitchen, absorbed the view from the window, then, slowly, for she was still stiff and weak, walked up the stairs and peered into the bathroom and lavatory. She exclaimed in horror at the sight of Colin's little hovel, but nodded with satisfaction at the other two bedrooms.

"Why doesn't she say something?" June asked her sister.

"It means she likes it," Mary said.

"Well, Brenda?" Dad cleared his throat. "What do you think? Nice place we've got here, eh?"

"It will do," Mrs Lockwood answered. "It will do." Then after a long pause she added "You've done wonders, considering. So many of our things here, and looking none the worse! I've got a very fine family." She rubbed a finger in the dust on the mantelpiece, and murmured, almost to herself, "Yes. Considering."

"Considering what, Mum?" Colin demanded. It made him feel cross: he had slaved all day humping furniture, and now she was about to find fault.

"The house was bombed, and . . ."

"You weren't here to supervise."

"Well, yes. Ron, I don't see any dusters or brooms or a Hoover. How are we going to keep the place clean?"

"I suppose I could ask Canon Brinkworth if we could borrow his," Mr Lockwood said.

"That's a good idea. Would you mind?"

"I shouldn't start spring-cleaning now, Brenda. You're not well enough."

"I'll just run it over the carpets."

"I'm going out," Colin said.

"Don't do that, dear. We've only been together, all of us, for five minutes out of the past forty-eight hours, and you want to run off."

"I said I'd meet Terry."

After he'd gone there was an awkward silence, then Mr Lockwood said, irritably, "Really, Brenda! You just don't know how to handle that boy! After all the work he's put in moving our things, and serving up all those hot meals yesterday!"

She sat down and sighed. "You're right, of course," she said. "I just feel very low . . . shock, perhaps. The hospital. Poor Lorna Wimbleball. I feel the slightest thing makes me snap."

"I'll do the hoovering," Mary said.

"No, you will not. You're more tired than anyone. It was silly of me to say anything about cleaning in the first place. What does the state of the carpet matter, or dusty mantelpieces, when half the city's been smashed and burned? I'll make us all a cup of tea, and we'll just sit and talk. June, love, I haven't heard half of your story yet."

"I'll make the tea," June said. "I know where everything is."

"Not too strong, dear. And two sugars for me."

"I *know*."

But before June had returned Mrs Lockwood had fallen asleep. Her dream was vivid and frightening. She was in the lift once more, but it was not the lift at Nimrod's; it was something much grander, with an attendant, and it was crowded with people. They were going down, as on the night of the blitz, but instead of being stranded between floors the lift stopped at the sixteenth. "Medicines and drugs," the attendant announced, and Colin, who was standing beside her, got out. "Come back!" she cried, but the lift was already in motion again. "Difference of generation," said Mrs Wimbleball. "Not the same values, Brenda dear, not the same concerns. Don't worry. It will be all right." But the lift was now crashing downwards out of control; people were being thrown sideways into each other: it can't be real, she said to herself; it's not really happening. She tried to scream. Her mouth opened, but no sound came out. Just before they hit the bottom of the shaft something stabbed her in the side: shrapnel.

She awoke with a start. "Tea's ready, Brenda!" Ron was prodding her. "You've been asleep for two hours. Mary's gone back to the hospital, so Colin has done the cooking; we didn't want to wake you up just to get a meal ready. It's fish and chips, surprise, surprise. And you will say it's excellent, do you hear? That's an order."

Oh, her family! They were marvellous; they rallied round in a crisis; who could want better kids, a kinder husband? She went into the kitchen, feeling a bit queasy. The dream, she told herself, had upset her. Why did she suddenly feel ill? Of course Colin's food (ugh!) was excellent . . . if only there wasn't so much grease on the chips . . . she could say she couldn't finish it because her injury had left her a bit shaken . . . one more chip . . .

She got up from the table, stumbled across the room, and leaned on the draining-board. She knew she was going to be sick.

At St David's Station the London train was about to depart. The platform was busy with people saying goodbye. From the carriage windows young men looked out; some of the families and girl-friends who were seeing them off were in tears. Many passengers were in uniform, and their kit-bags cluttered the corners of the train's corridors, but others wore civilian clothes, and their possessions filled suitcases and hold-alls: recent recruits, those who a short while back had received their call-up papers. A few joked with the people on the platform, told them not to be silly, there was nothing to worry about. Maybe Hitler had, after all, missed the bus. No-one was going to be sent immediately to the front line in Libya or Burma, or be shot down the day after tomorrow over Hamburg. But some did not know how to say farewell to wife, girl-friend or mother, just stood there unsuccessfully searching for anything to say that had significance.

Lars leaned out of the window, hands on Mary's shoulders, stroking her hair. "I'll write as soon as I get there," he said. "From somewhere in the south of England, as the newsreels say. I don't even know exactly where I'm going."

Mary nodded. "You could phone, perhaps."

"Shall I? I won't know where you'll be."

"The hospital. Leave a message to ring back, with the number, and a time."

"All right." They were silent a moment. "Goodbye means God be with you," he said. "It doesn't mean we'll never see each other again."

"No, of course not."

"You're a sensible girl, Mary."

It was hard, very hard, not to open the door and climb in beside him, travel to . . . where? The sunset, like film-lovers. A grey dawn, the wail of shells. Being sensible was the hardest thing in the world.

The train started, so slowly at first that for a fraction of a second its movement was imperceptible. It was like a snail, slower than walking-pace: travel by snail, she thought wildly, as Lars leaned further out and kissed her; now she was walking quite quickly trying to make the moment last, no, not for ever, but as long as it was possible: she was running, trying to imprint on her mind the smell of his face, the rough skin of his cheek, the laughter-lines when he smiled, the exact blueness of his eyes, the precise shade of the straw-coloured hair.

"Goodbye! Goodbye!" The train had beaten her, inevitably, and she stood near the end of the platform, waving; the carriages curved round, dwindled, and now his head was a dot. The guard's van grew smaller and disappeared. Rails narrowed into the distance. Smoke drifting from the engine thinned and vanished as smoke always did after a light has died.

She walked back into the city. It was unlikely she would ever see him again. He had not said he loved her. Not a hint of a thought or a feeling on that subject had been mentioned. Only once had there been anything in his kisses. Young men and women liked to go out together, play with hands and hair, wind arms round one another, kiss: it did not necessarily signify anything. Mostly, in fact, it did not, particularly now in this war-time when death sometimes seemed a more frequent fact than love. Some did say "I love you" and it was a lie; maybe it was natural or expected at a certain moment; maybe it was pure selfishness. Love certainly was more, possibly something quite else, than saying "I love you".

She felt incredibly empty. A light had died. Exactly, she thought, like the ruined streets through which she was walking. Despite all the optimism, the newspaper reports of "undamaged morale", the heart of the city of Exeter had perished, perhaps for ever. A middle-aged couple had been killed in that house; a child from that one had lost the sight of both eyes; a woman over there had been mutilated by shrapnel; an elderly man in the shop on the corner had been crushed by falling debris.

Several churches had been destroyed. The top of the tower of one of them had been sliced off, horizontally, exposing the bells to the wind and the weather, and St Sidwell's had lost its west front: looking into it was like staring into the throat of a giant fish. The books in the public library were still burning. The probate registry had received a direct hit; six hundred years of private and public history lay in ashes. In places where the rubble had not yet been cleared, steel girders wound and bent as if they were made of plasticine; a few walls stood, their windows just gaping squares, around them a desert of stone and plaster. Electric light wires and telephone lines were tangled in grotesque knots, their poles tottering at weird angles, missing insulators like empty sockets in rows of teeth. Half-damaged buildings curiously reminded her of people. One whose roof had fallen in looked squashed, its windows flattened and crooked, like a man who has been hit on the head so brutally that his eyes bulged out. Any broken window was a face with a shattered eye, a blown-off door a mouth open with shock. One house had tilted sideways into another; it was a woman fainting on a man's shoulder. Everywhere missing arms, sagging jaws, men on crutches, lunatics: that was what whole streets resembled. Screams of agony, frozen in stone.

There was her work at the hospital to absorb her. She would put Lars out of her mind, throw herself into a round of endless duties. But I am empty: she wanted to shriek the words at the sky. Love me, please. Empty.

Colin woke earlier than he had expected; it was the brilliant light of a summer morning preparing for a day of heat. It did not matter: this Saturday he had intended an early start; he was going fishing with his new rod, going to show Terry how it was done. His tiny bedroom was still the way he wanted it, a mattress on the floor and himself in a sleeping-bag. The walls were bare except for a painting of a woman riding a motorbike which he had found in a junk cupboard at school. Paul Sanders, mason, lay on the window-sill. Dad had discovered it the night before last, and despite Colin's protests, had insisted on returning it to the cathedral. He was not very happy, he said, about having a thief for a son: the Dean would have to know about it. However, much to Mr Lockwood's surprise the Dean said Colin could keep it. The monument had been so badly smashed that restoration work was considered impossible. "Nevertheless," Dad said, "you can write a letter of apology for taking it in the first place. You could have had it easily enough by just asking. I don't know; sometimes I think you're a complete idiot." Colin wrote the letter without any argument, grateful that he would not have to keep the piece of marble hidden now. He wondered why he had become so attached to the thing; it was quite irrational: Paul Sanders, mason, was, he supposed, like a talisman, maybe even a comforter, serving a function similar to a child's dummy.

From two floors below came the gentle twangling of a harpsichord. It was the old Canon's; he often played it, particularly in the morning. It was a pleasant soothing sound in the distance, bedtime music rather than a dawn chorus. A German composer, Colin remembered, one of the Bachs perhaps, had written a long piece for the harpsichord because some important person had ordered it specially; this person was a raving insomniac, and the music was supposed to send him to sleep. This, yes, it was the same piece: Mick Revell, the music master, had played a gramophone record of it in class. It hadn't sent Colin to sleep. He hadn't said so to anyone, but he was forced to admit to himself that he rather liked it. The Goldberg Variations: that was the title. Funny how you could hear each individual string on a harpsichord, every plucking twang and vibration, not like the smooth clean action of a piano's hammers.

Bach was a German. From that country came sweet and beautiful sounds. And high explosive bombs that smashed buildings and killed or maimed people. Strange.

This room was all right. Mum had made a few adverse comments, particularly about the woman on the motorbike, who was wearing very few clothes, but she had not insisted on him removing it from the wall. Life with his mother was often a battle, but, he thought, it usually ended in a draw. He was glad she was home, really glad that she was safe and well; life without her was impossible to imagine.

Today would be fun. He was taking Terry up the river, to his own secret spot, a little hide-out about a mile upstream above the weirs. It wasn't really his own, of course, but he had always called it his. It was so well-hidden by bushes that no-one had ever disturbed him there. Later, after fishing, they could swim if the day was very hot; it was good to race against the current and reach the overhanging branch on the opposite bank in the shortest possible time and distance. Then, tonight, they were going out with a couple of girls. For him, the first time ever: his stomach lurched uncomfortably at the thought of it, and his heart beat faster. They had met yesterday evening, when he and Terry were loafing about on the quay, and somehow they had struck up a conversation; after three quarters of an hour of chat and banter, Janet and Lorraine had agreed to come out with them. Maybe they wouldn't turn up. But probably they would.

He got out of bed and dressed, thinking thoughts he found himself surprised at daring to think: the blitz had not been all disaster. If it had not happened he wouldn't have made friends with Terry, or slept in the hay-loft, cooked the fish, picked up the girls: it had opened a new phase of his life, freer, more exciting than the one that had closed. But prison gates were trying to keep him from it, having to go to school in John Alderdyce's ridiculous uniform, for instance. Soon, in a week or so, everything would be normal again, dull and monotonous, unless he really fought to be himself. He was determined not to let the prison-gates shut on him, ever again. It was almost a pity the blitz hadn't been worse, hadn't devastated the routine of life completely, made it quite impossible to live as once he had done. He would not give in, become a boring salesman or rep or insurance clerk when he left school. He'd like to do . . . what? Sea and surf, follow the sun round the world, or be a lumber-jack in Canada, rule a tropical island and have a hundred and fifty bare-bosomed wives. But if the war continued he'd be called up and possibly end up with a bullet in his head at the age of eighteen. Nothing achieved, no worthwhile living ever done.

He went downstairs. Mum and June were still sleeping; Dad would already have gone to work. He put a kettle on the stove for tea, and gave himself his usual Saturday treat: a boiled egg. He sat by the window in the living-room, eating his breakfast, staring out across the green of the Close at the cathedral. The only damage visible on this side of the building was to the windows; they had all been boarded up. Otherwise it was its usual self, resplendent in the early light, the towers dazzling in the sun, their weather-vanes glittering gold pennants. It had endured. It had given two fingers to Hitler. Six centuries it had stood. One little Austrian maniac might have ordered its cancellation, but he had failed. There it stood. He had not realised before how important the cathedral was to him. He did not love it in the same way as his father did; it was, simply, that Exeter was inconceivable without it. A few nights back there had been a possibility it would end, and that was a dark thought indeed. But like the city and its survivors, like him, it was there.

An hour later he and Terry were at the secret spot, the hide-out, fishing. Poaching, to be accurate, but it was virtually impossible that anyone should see them. Colin sang as he cast his line:

"Cape Cod girls they have no combs,
Heave away! Heave away!
They comb their hair with cod-fish bones,
And they're bound for Australia!"

"We could camp here on warm nights," Terry said. "Fried fish for breakfast."

"Another great idea from Terry Wootton. You're a genius."

"And modest with it."

"Let's see if the girls agree about that."

"Got us a date, didn't it? Can't beat us Londoners for a bit of the old one-two."

"Which do you prefer?"

"The dark-haired bit of skirt. Janet."

"We shan't fall out, then."

"Why? You like the little blonde?"

"Lorraine. Yes. I do."

"You're sex-mad."

"So? Anyway, speak for yourself."

"I am!"

"Well," said Colin, looking down-river through the trees, "half a cheer for Hitler, I say."

"What do you mean?"

"Oh . . . that's too complicated to explain." At this distance the city looked undamaged, looked as it always had done, a tired grey slope of houses surmounted by two towers, in a dip between hillsides. It would be renewed, made whole. "It's like the phoenix," he said. "It will rise from its ashes."

"You sound like some pansy poncy poet. What are you talking about?"

"Exeter. It's a place *worth* talking about."

116